As Angels Weep

The unauthorized reproduction or distribution of this copyrighted work is illegal. Criminal copyright infringement (including infringement without monetary gain) is investigated by the FBI and is punishable by up to 5 years in federal prison and a fine of $250,000.

Please purchase only authorized electronic editions and do not participate in, or encourage, the electronic piracy of copyrighted materials. Your support of the author's rights is appreciated.

This book is a work of fiction. Names, characters, places, and incidents are the products of the author's imagination or used fictitiously. Any resemblance to actual events, locales or persons, living or dead, is entirely coincidental.

As Angels Weep-Supernatural Penance
Copyright © 2012 by Kali Willows
ISBN-13: 978-1507539774
ISBN-10: 1507539770

Cover art by Kali Willows / Kinderd Productions

All rights reserved. Except for use in any review, the reproduction or utilization of this work, in whole or in part, in any form by any electronic, mechanical or other means now known or hereafter invented, is forbidden without the written permission of the publisher.

Published by Kali Willows

Look for us online at:
www.kaliwillows.com

DEDICATION

For my Becca,

May your wings be vast
And golden and your spirit soar.
Thank you
For all you have given.

PREFACE

PENANCE was inconsequential to me once upon a time. For the first time in my life, it means everything. My soul depends on it. For years, I swindled wealthy women, made shady business deals that caused harm to others. In just seven days, I face spiritual exile. Doomed to purgatory for my past deeds and failure to live my humanity. My one chance at salvation? I have one assignment to complete, with rules, very strict rules, and unspeakable consequences if I fail. Whoever said good guys finish last was sadly mistaken. I'd never been a good guy. Now, I have to be one if I want redemption.

"It's not the time we have in life.
It's what we do with it,
and the impact we have on others.
That is our true legacy."

Kali Willows

AS ANGELS WEEP

Supernatural Penance

By Kali Willows

Chapter One

BRIGHTNESS penetrated his eyelids.

"Jasmine, turn the damn light off." Luther called to his girlfriend lying beside him and buried his face into the pillow as he grumbled.

The bed shook hard.

He bolted upright and gasped. "Earthquake."

The tremors stopped, and a golden hue flooded the room.

"What the hell?" A dream? He wiped the corners of his eyes with his fingertips, fighting the blurry vision as he struggled to wake from his deep slumber.

"Luther, I bring you a message." A tall, dark, ominous figure with wings stood beside the bed. The bulky hood of a cloak concealed his face. Luther tensed as panic flooded him.

"Who the hell are you? How did you get into my house?" He scrambled for the cordless phone on the nightstand, but it had vanished. He scanned the room. Zilch. Left with no way to call for help, he shuddered from the daggers of fear jabbing through his chest.

"Your time draws short; you must change your life path or suffer the wrath of God."

"Crap. This is one of those screwed up dreams again." He ran his fingers through his hair and tried to will himself awake. "Didn't I already dream this last week and a few times before that?"

"You are not delusional at this moment, nor the many times before. You have failed to heed my warnings. It is the final time I offer you salvation if you choose to adhere to my words of caution."

"This is messed up." He shook his head and blinked hard.

"This...is a premonitory message. Your philandering and greed has caused many others great pain. Change your ways or you forfeit your life, forever in the hereafter."

"Forfeit? Okay, sure. This can't be real. Maybe I shouldn't have eaten that sandwich before bed. I should know better. Gives me nightmares." He shook his groggy head. "Hey, Jazzy, wake up. I need you to pinch me or something. I'm in the middle of another weird dream." He looked to his side, where she lay sound asleep.

"You have one final chance to change your destiny," the hooded figure roared. "If you wrong another person, you will die and your soul will be sentenced to purgatory for all eternity."

Luther wiggled his fingers and toes. "I can feel my body; my dreams aren't this vivid." He looked at his hands and then back to the towering man beside the bed. "Right, purgatory. Got it, and your name again?"

"I am Jeremiel, Archangel of God's Mercy. The one who brings caution. The next messenger, if you fail to alter your ways, will be Azrael."

"Azrael...the Angel of Death?"

"Archangel, yes."

"Okay, if this is real, then what's with the sad get up?" He tittered and pointed at the old robe covering his antagonist. "Wouldn't angels have, I don't know, a golden halo or even some fancy digs?" He scrubbed his face then paused. "Wait a minute, is this a joke? Did she put you up to this? Jasmine, wake up." He leaned over and shook her shoulder. "Jasmine."

She rolled to her side and didn't bother to open her eyes. "What is it, Luther?"

"Who is this clown?" He motioned over to the side of his bed, to what somehow changed to an empty space in their very dark room.

"That's nice, honey. I told you not to snack before bed." She let out a big yawn and turned over again as she pulled the blanket up to her chin. "Go back to sleep."

He reached for the light on his nightstand and grabbed the cord. Luther felt his way up to the switch along the cool, smooth plastic, and then...bare wire?

A sudden jolt shot through him. Sparks flew from his fingertips where they met the exposed metal strands. His entire body went rigid with buzzing agony. The voltage stopped, and he collapsed back into his pillow.

His heart pummeled his chest. He took inventory of his hand, arm, and body. "Holy shit."

In a rush of terror, he jumped out of bed and scampered over to the wall. He flicked on the ceiling light and he scanned the room. The spot where he'd seen the tall figure stood empty. The lamp showed no damage from the electrical surge. The noxious odor of burned hair filled his nostrils and turned his stomach, but there was no visible smoke in the air.

Back at the nightstand, he inspected the faulty cord. Luther had felt the exposed wire, but inch-by-inch, he scrutinized the entire length from base to the plug in the wall and found nothing wrong with the lamp.

Jasmine slept soundly. His heart raced.

***

"I CAN have dinner ready for you when you get home tonight. I'll be finished early at the clinic." Jasmine placed his coffee on the table in front of him. "We can spend a little quality time, and maybe talk?"

With each flip of the newspaper pages, he avoided eye contact and gave a flat voice, "Don't bother. I have to work late at the office."

"Again? That's the fourth night this week, Luther." The spoon clunked in the sink, stirring him from his focus on the New York stock market section.

"What do you expect? My clients' needs don't just exist between eight and five, Monday through Friday."

"I'm sure they are supposed to have some kind of a life outside of Wall Street, too."

"Are you getting cranky again?" He laughed and turned the page.

"You could at least have the decency to look at me when you brush me off."

"Um hmm." He trolled down the columns of promising numbers.

"That's it." She threw a rolled up tea towel at him. It hit his paper and tore it straight down the middle. Hatred flashed in Jasmine's eyes then she stormed out the kitchen.

"Hey?" he called after her.

Guess I'd better go see what mood swing has hit her. Luther got to his feet and followed her down the hall and up the long, winding staircase. Through the ajar door, he peered and shook his head at the sight of the open suitcase on the bed. This time, she was serious. What could have her so riled up?

"So, where is it you're off to, sweetums?" He leaned against the doorframe and tucked his hands in his pockets.

"Don't call me that. Your sexy little smile isn't gonna cut it this time." She yanked the bureau drawer open, and it fell on the floor. "Great," she rumbled as she crouched down and scooped the contents up.

"What? Why are you so angry? Because I read the newspaper?"

"Oooo—" Jasmine growled and stomped back to the bed with an armful of clothes and flung them into the suitcase. "You infuriate me."

"I can think of something else I do to you, baby." He strolled up to her with confidence. Luther gripped her hips from behind. In a bid to curtail her rage, he nuzzled his nose into the nape of her neck and blazed a trail of playful nibbles along her skin.

She tried to resist his charms, but that lasted all of a second or two. Before she could come to her senses, he tightened his grip.

"Come on, baby, you know you can't stay mad at me." He continued to devour her neck, running his fingers inside her blouse.

"Stop it. You're such an ass." She tried to pull away, but he held her close.

"I haven't gotten to the best part yet." He handled her hips and coaxed her around to face him.

"What?" she snapped.

"I got somethin' for ya, Jazz." He slid one hand down the front of his dress pants while the other still held her close.

"You think sex fixes everything, don't you?"

"Well, it helps, but I had a different idea in mind." Frowning at her fiery glare while he reached into his pocket.

"Stop it. It's not gonna work this time. I'm too mad." She pushed against his chest, and he went down on one knee with a grin.

"Jazzy, don't leave me. I love you." He pulled out a black velvet box and held it up to her.

Her ice blue eyes softened as the tears welled up. "That isn't funny."

Without a word, Luther remained on one knee as he gazed up at her. He fashioned his most persuasive stare. To flash her the puppy dog eyes had become his favorite trick in desperate times. He opened the box and revealed the two-karat marvel he held onto for weeks.

***

THROUGH his massive office window, Luther surveyed the gloomy sky that cast a dark shadow over the sea of Manhattan buildings. In the plush comfort of the leather chair, he eased back, pleased with himself. He tossed the sealed package across the desk to his colleague and gave a chuckle of amusement. "Here's your cut of the Foley deal."

"You managed to wrap this one up quick." Marvin offered a tight grin.

"Yeah, well, she didn't want her husband to find out she got screwed."

"Which kind of screwed?" His business partner grinned.

"Both. In fact, I had your share ready a few days ago. Where did you take off to?"

"I...had some personal matters to attend."

"Is Beth okay?"

"Never better." Marvin shifted in his chair and stifled a cough. "So, what about this thing with you and Jasmine last night, she agreed?"

"You sound surprised? She's been beggin' for a diamond ring for years."

"So why did you go through with it? Have you changed your mind?" His partner tore the envelope open and counted the wad of cash.

"Hell no, but it buys me some time. The rock on her finger is enough to calm her for a while. Thanks to good old Sandra Foley for that bling."

"I don't get it, Luther." He shook his head.

"What's to get? Some serious strings were pulled to get her."

"I remember well." He tilted his head back with a smirk then glanced at Luther with pursed lips. "Why the hell would you ask a girl to marry you if you don't want to get married?"

"Whoa there, cowboy. I never said I *asked* her anything."

"You gave her an engagement ring, right?"

"The trick is, I got down on one knee and held the rock up. I never said a word, and I *never* asked her to marry me."

"Wow, you could justify selling a sheep to the lions, couldn't you?" He tucked the bundle of money into his suit coat pocket.

"It made her happy, didn't it? She'll hang around a while longer."

"Why keep yourself tied down? You're a wealthy, successful, handsome guy who could have any woman you want, and I mean *any woman*."

"I don't want to let her go. We have good times together. She's got an incredible body, and she's a minx in the sack. Dating while you're single means fending off gold-diggers who expect something. Jazz is cool."

"She can't be that cool if you still screw other women."

"Sure she can. But why give up the dream when I can live large?"

"So, you're not getting hitched?"

"Uh, no!"

"That's a relief."

"Why?"

"Because you're my idol, Luther. You have the bachelor life I've always dreamed about, and if you take vows, I can't live vicariously through your escapades anymore."

"You're not so monogamous yourself, you sly dog."

"What?" He raised his brows as he hunched his shoulders.

"I saw you sneak into Kimberly's car the other night."

"Well, my conquests are small potatoes compared to you," he huffed. "My mother came to town for a visit. She and Beth went to a gala that night, so I had a little fun." Marvin unbuttoned his jacket and rested his arm over the back of the leather office chair.

"Why did she leave so soon? Beth said she planned to stay a few weeks to look into buying a condo here."

"Mother? Uh, she had...some medical issues to address. The real estate didn't suit her needs right at the present."

"I hope not too serious?"

A slight tilt of his lips, Marvin tapped his finger against his chin before he answered. "Nothing terminal."

Marvin cleared his throat and reached into the other side of his coat. Muffled crinkling filled the material as he dug in, then pulled out some wrapped stogies. "Here's a present for you, bro. Enjoy."

Luther accepted them and opened the cigar box on his desk. "You keep me well stocked. What's the special occasion this time?"

"Can't a guy get a gift for his buddy when he travels without the third degree?" He guffawed.

Luther pulled out two of the Cubans and handed one to his partner.

"It's okay, I still have mine." Marvin held out a half-burned cigar for him to light.

"You've traveled a lot. It'll take me a year to smoke all of these. I'll have to return the favor soon."

"No worries," Marvin said. With a wink and passive wave of his hand, he dismissed the acknowledgement. "Soon enough."

Luther pulled out his trusty Zippo lighter, bent over the desk, flipped open the metal lid, clicked the flint, and held it. He lit his partner's first and watched him inhale deep, releasing a thick cloud of the sweet, musky smoke. "Good times, buddy."

"I still can't believe you got away with it, and she never found out after all this time."

"Yeah, I'm that good." Luther sat back to light his own cigar. As he flicked the lint again, a thunderous crack erupted, and a huge flame exploded in front of him that sent him coiling back in his leather chair. He toppled over and landed ass first on the floor.

"What the f—?" He jumped up and grabbed his glass of water from the desk and doused the flames that ate his newest contracts.

A soppy pile of cindered paperwork filled his desk. He picked up the lifeless lighter and examined it. At arm's length, he held it and turned his head a little. He flinched as he lit again. No thunderous noise, and the normal flame danced gracefully from the device.

He stared at the light in disbelief as it flickered, catching the surprise in Marvin's face as he stood behind his own chair.

Chapter Two

THE DELICIOUS aroma of roasted prime rib filled the regal dining room of the Evan's estate as Sarah; the maid, served Luther and his father, Jasper. They sat, for most of the meal, in silence. The occasional scrapes of their silver forks and knives over the bone china echoed throughout the sparse room.

"So, I hear you asked Jasmine's hand in marriage at last." The teacup jittered on the saucer as his father placed it on the dinner table with his shaky hand.

"Uh, I guess I did." Luther wiped the corners of his mouth and flung the napkin onto his half-emptied plate. *Here it comes.* He sighed.

"When is the date? I can check with my assistant, Alice, and reserve the church—"

"No!"

"Why not?" His voice remained steady while he called Luther's bluff, as usual.

"We haven't set a date. We just got engaged four days ago." The chair's cushion grew restrictive, as did the line of questioning. He shifted and adjusted his position, still uncomfortable under his father's penetrating gaze.

"Uh huh."

"Come on, Dad. What's the big deal? We haven't even finalized the details yet."

"And your view on having children with her, has that suddenly changed as well?"

Heavy thrumming of his own heartbeat filled Luther's ears from the deafening quiet filling the length of the formal dining room. Jasper glanced over Luther's shoulder to the wall behind him and stared. The wall held but one thing to capture his attention that way. The massive painted portrait of his beloved mother. A grimace filled his father's withered face.

"Marriage isn't to be taken lightly, son. It's to build a life together, to make a commitment of eternal love."

"That's not news to me, Dad. I knew you were gonna nag me about this."

"Oh, and what am I nagging about?" He eased his chair back from the table and rang the little silver service bell sitting in front of his dinner plate.

Cramps in Luther's stomach came on suddenly, so intense he hunched over. "You've wanted me to get hitched for the last five years. I gave her the ring. You're still not happy?" The pain deepened, and he shoved his chair back to get up. "Excuse me." He stormed down the hallway to the bathroom.

After a few editions of Forbes magazine to bide his time, the physical discomfort lessened, but the occasional spasm still rolled over him. Hesitant to listen to anymore of his father's lectures, he returned to the dining room.

"Sorry, Dad. My stomach is upset. I can't eat anymore." Without waiting for a response, he left his father at the table and went into the next room. The maid passed him on her way to see his father.

On Luther's coattails, through the doorway, Jasper called back to the maid. "Sarah, thank you for dinner. We'll have our Brandy in the parlor now."

"Very well, Mr. Evans."

"I hope you aren't ill, son. You look pale." As he stood at the entrance, his concerned voice grabbed Luther's attention.

"Maybe I've been a little off this week." Sweat erupted in a thick layer over his scalp and face. It streamed along his forehead, trailed down his temples, and over his throat.

"Your walking out on people in the middle of a conversation has become a rude habit I'm not fond of." He wobbled in, leaning heavy on his cane as he moved over to his armchair and sat.

"Then maybe people should stay out of things that aren't their business."

"Sit down." His strict tone held admonishment.

Luther complied, planting himself in the opposing wing-backed chair to face his external conscience—the only one he had.

"Don't you grow tired of the façade?"

"What?"

"You don't love her."

"That's not true."

"Not enough, then. She deserves more than you give her."

"Hey, I give her plenty. She has no complaints."

"I don't mean the material needs. I'm talking about your heart, your dedication, children...the kind of love you would give up your life for."

"That doesn't exist."

"It did for me." His father held up his hand and flashed his worn wedding band.

"Sure, and look where it got you, in a big, empty house with nothing but a bum leg." He motioned with his hands around the room.

"I have you."

"A grown man, who comes to dinner once in a while?"

"Your drinks." The maid entered the room, a silver dish in hand with the full crystal bottle and two goblets.

"Thank you, Sarah. That will be all."

"Yes, sir." Smiling, she placed the tray on the table and left them alone.

"Yes, about dinner, why don't you bring Jasmine by anymore?"

"She's busy."

"Too busy to celebrate with her father-in-law to be? I don't think so."

"What do you want from me?" he groaned. Uncomfortable tingles formed in his fingers. Luther wrung his hands and cracked his knuckles, trying to get his circulation back.

"I want you to do what's right. We both know you don't intend to walk down the aisle. You haven't even stopped dating other women, despite that you live in sin."

Luther couldn't rebuke his observation, his dad was right.

"Son, I know how we lost your mother hurt you a lot. But you don't honor her memory by a proposal to your lady done like a business deal."

"What do you know about my feelings, Dad? You never asked me. You went on as though it never happened, sermons every Sunday, you continue to force a fake smile, and after twenty years, you still wear that gold band." He leaned forward as he leered at his father's left hand. He grabbed the bottle, pulled the stopper out, and poured the aged liquor for each of them.

"I continued to live because it's what she wanted for the both of us." He collected the glass Luther held up for him.

"You're so delusional, Dad."

"Mind your tongue, son." He narrowed his eyes, his voice sounding gruff.

"I'm sorry. It's just that...how would you know what she wanted? It's not like she had a chance to sit down and sort it all out."

"When you were born, we both agreed, no matter what, we would embrace our faith and live life to its fullest, for you."

"Too bad the drunk driver had a different idea, or was that out of your God's hands, too?"

"He is also your God."

"I wouldn't say that."

"To renounce your faith is an angry response that should have played itself out years ago."

"Yeah, well, maybe it's just self-preservation." Luther sipped from the glass. "Your God gave me a beautiful reminder of that night, to match the leg you'll never fully walk on ever again." He raked his fingers through his hair, over the deep, pitted scar across the side of his scalp he managed to hide from the world. "What was it, twenty stitches and two weeks in ICU?"

"I'm at a loss. I don't know how to help you through this anymore."

"I don't need any help. I'm happy with how my life is. I have all I want, a mansion, a sports car, money, and I did it all on my own with hard work and determination. I didn't rely on prayers to reach my goals."

In silence, his dad's smoldering glare burrowed through Luther's hardened exterior. His cheeks burned.

"I have no regrets," Luther bantered.

"That's disappointing."

"What is?"

"Your lack of remorse. From what I hear around town, you've done plenty you should be sorry for." His dad tapped his finger on the top of his cane.

"I haven't hurt anyone." He looked out the window to avoid his father's piercing stare.

"My parishioners tell me otherwise."

"Your par—? Are you kidding me? You believe idle gossip over my word?" He shook his head and shot a defiant gape at his father.

"I believe there are a number of local women reeling financially, who've lost their assets and their marriages, thanks to you."

"So, I get all the credit for *their* indiscretions?"

"Yes, you do. More than ever when the meager praying you do these days is preying on the kindness of desolate women, when you swindle their hearts and their money on bad investments."

"It's just business. They know the risks. I can't take what they don't want to give."

"Continue to tell yourself that. Maybe one day you'll actually believe it."

To bite his tongue wouldn't have been any more painful than the pangs of shame shooting through his chest.

"None of it's as bad as the stunt you pulled on Jasmine though."

"What?"

"At the start of your relationship."

"What do you know?" His pulse raced.

"I know you robbed her of truth and happiness."

Luther sighed in irritation before bantering back. "More gossip from your congregation?"

"What you did was...unconscionable."

"What in particular is it you think I did, Dad?" Curiosity about how much he knew quickly overrode the need to avoid the topic all together. "Never mind. Maybe coming for dinner isn't such a good idea anymore."

"So, you think if you cut your father off, it will solve everything? I'm the only family you have left. It's time you start behaving like it."

"Lay off the lectures and I might come around more often." He focused out the window at the monstrous weeping willow swaying in the breeze.

"Very well, then. You'll have to face the consequences sooner or later. I'll be here if you need me."

"Thank you." He huffed with relief.

"Just remember, son, if you don't right your wrongs soon, you will be judged by God, and then Heaven help you."

Luther held in his snigger of amusement as he shook his head. "You never change, Dad." He held up his glass and toasted his father.

"I truly hope someday, son, you do." Jasper shifted in his seat and grimaced.

"What's wrong?" He sat forward and touched his father's knee.

His dad took a few long, deep breaths and rubbed his chest, and then his arm. "Probably just gas. It will pass. It always does."

Chapter Three

"I'M SERIOUS, Jocelyn, this deal can't be beat. I'm gonna make you a fortune." Luther surveyed his own devilish reflection in the mirrored backsplash of the bar as he poured the champagne. After spraying on his special batch of Giorgio Armani he hid in his office, he snuck over for a quick rendezvous with his newest victim—uh, *client*.

"I'm worried Justin will find out."

"I swear, sweetheart, you'll be tanning under the Tuscan sun before he even knows what hit him." Handing her the crystal flute, he clinked glasses with her as he eyed her soft pink satin and black lace attire. He licked his lips at the vision of her heaving mounds of creamy flesh.

"You sure make that bed look inviting." Luther nodded to the down filled pillows and strewn bedspread behind her. He gulped his drink and set the glass on the nightstand. He hovered over his prey. "When's he due home?" He captured her free hand, slid it down his stomach and over his zipper.

"In a few hours. His plane lands at eight-thirty."

"Hmmm, plenty of time." His hand over hers, he cupped her fingers while she kneaded his hungry flesh.

She set her glass down and tugged at his belt with impatience. He ran his fingers through her platinum mass of curls, seized a fistful and pulled her head back as he captured her lips. To move in for the kill, he grabbed a condom from his pocket and dropped his pants to the floor. He pulled his half-buttoned shirt over his head between kisses, and mounted her in a rush.

After a few minutes of foreplay, he noticed something different—his usually eager libido wouldn't cooperate. His semi-erection before he undressed had dissipated and didn't come back. Luther ground his hips against her, hoping the friction would arouse him. But his excitement never piqued. This didn't make sense. A smokin' hot woman with sexy curves, not hard on the eyes at all. She didn't even talk too much. So why in hell couldn't he get hard?

"Hey, babe, how about you do me a favor first?" He rolled over onto his back and pulled her hand down to his limp biscuit. "Suck me off."

Compliant and determined, she went to work and used every imaginable oral talent. No matter what she did, he couldn't get an erection.

"You aren't attracted to me?" She gazed up with tear-filled eyes as her chin quivered.

"Of course I am. Shit, this has never happened to me before." He clamped his hands over his face with frustration.

"I have an idea. Justin needs a little pharmaceutical help sometimes. Do you wanna try one?" She reached over, pulled the drawer open, and presented a prescription bottle to him.

"Viagra? You've gotta be kidding me. I'm thirty-five." Insult added to injury, he sat up and collected his clothes.

"Please, baby, I want you so bad. Do it for me?" she begged as she rubbed his bare chest. He paused with anticipation, the light scraping of her nails down the plains of his abdomen hindering his refusal.

With a grimace, he dropped his clothes and held his hand out. "Gimme a drink to wash it down with."

***

AN HOUR and two Viagra later, nothing had changed—except he was on his way home, unsuccessful with his conquest, humiliated and perturbed.

Unbelievable. He shook his head. Pulling up to the entrance in his convertible, he punched in his security code. After the massive wrought iron gate opened, he drove up and parked in the garage. The lemon-scented wet wipes he kept in the middle console were for just such an occasion. He took one out and swabbed away the implicating cologne as he checked in the rearview mirror for any signs of lipstick or marks.

Satisfied he would pass inspection, he gathered his briefcase, overcoat and went inside, hoping for a quick shower and an early night. The house sat quiet in the dark. Maybe Jasmine went out with her friends. That would save him the grief of explaining his late arrival, once again.

Drained, he dropped his coat and briefcase on the bench in the hall. He went into the living room, and the lights flashed on.

"Surprise!" a crowd of people roared.

"What the—?" He grabbed his chest in shock. Thirty or so friends and colleagues surrounded him with confetti and balloons they tossed around the room.

"Welcome home, baby." Jasmine threw her arms around his neck. She squeezed him tight and planted a lingering kiss on him. In a slow retreat, she stared at him with wide eyes.

"What?" he scoffed.

She brought her hands to her sides and stepped back. At first, tears collected in her eyes as she glanced at the floor and shook her head.

"What?" He grew impatient with her silence.

Jasmine looked up at him and furrowed her brows as she inspected him. "Hey, why is your face so red and puffy? Are you okay?"

"What is this?" he whispered through clenched teeth.

"Come on, bro, you didn't think you could pull one over on us, did you?" Stephan from the office strolled up to him and slapped him on the shoulder with a big grin. "You got engaged and didn't tell us?"

"Jazz, why did you do this?" Unable to hide his annoyance, he ground his teeth as he glared at her.

Jasmine gave a rigid grin that failed to reach her eyes. "I didn't. They surprised me just as much as they did you." The unmistakable hurt in her eyes caught him. "I had planned on dinner in for us. Remember? We were supposed to talk tonight."

"Come on, have a drink and tell us all about how you proposed." Stephan threw his arm around him and led him to the billiards room.

One person after another came up and gave congratulations and hugs. Halfway through the crowd, his head started to hurt, and a very unexpected issue popped up—the Viagra kicked in, both of them.

"Wow, Luther, I know this is exciting, but can you put that thing away?" Another buddy snickered as he walked by. Before he could do an about face to hide behind the bar, every jaw in the room dropped and all eyes fell to his arousal, much to his dismay. He grabbed a platter of cheese, clumsily dumped the food on the counter, and used the metal to shield his ragging hard-on.

"Jasmine, looks like your fiancé needs a little attention," one voice called out, and the room burst into laughter.

"Oh, yeah, that's funny. Thanks, Johnny," he growled. The pounding of his heart grew heavier.

"Everyone, please, join us in the dining room. There's a wonderful spread of food for you to enjoy," Marvin called out and met Luther's gaze.

"Thank you," he mouthed.

The crowd cleared out of the room, their laughter along with them. He crouched over with discomfort.

Holy crap, this is starting to hurt.

"Mind telling me what's got you so excited, *dear?*" Fury creased the corners or her eyes. Her forced voice seized his attention. She knew something was up—besides the bald avenger.

"I don't know. I guess…celebrating our love?"

"Sure, that sounds about right." She folded her arms across her chest and glowered at him. He could have sworn daggers shot out of her eyes. To evoke her fiery temper had never been a good thing. He had to think quickly.

"I, uh…I—"

"Oh, I got it." She shot him a blazing scowl. "I could smell your Armani and lemon."

"No, Jazz, that's not it. I-I had a headache at the office. Marvin had already left, and I needed some aspirin. I found a bottle in his desk and took two pills. I didn't read the label." Fast talk was his mastered survival tool.

"You expect me to believe that? The man who refuses to take any medication?"

"Uh, Jasmine, it's true." Marvin sped into the room and looked to Luther. "I have a bottle of—"

"Viagra," Luther blurted out.

"Right, Viagra. I have a prescription. I keep it in my desk at work." He rushed to Luther's side.

"Because you have such a great need for it at your desk, right?" she goaded him.

"No, of course not. Uh…Beth doesn't know I need it. I'm—"

"Embarrassed. He was too embarrassed to tell his wife he was having trouble." Luther raised his brows, convinced he would get out of this mess with his puppy dog eyes, but his vision blurred.

"Right," she scoffed.

"No, Jasmine, I swear it to you on my mother's grave."

"Your mother is alive and well in Montana, Marvin."

"Yes, of course," he cleared his throat. "But I swear it. Please don't tell Beth."

The pair stood side-by-side with their persuasive pleas. Luther's hard-on grew even more painful, and his chest started to hurt. Dizziness took hold, and the room started to spin.

"Luther, are you alright?"

***

"YOU SHOULD be fine, Mr. Evans, but I wouldn't recommend anymore medication without a doctor's prescription." The salt-and-pepper haired gentleman removed his stethoscope and tucked it into his lab coat pocket. He yanked the plaid curtain open—the other three hospital beds in the emergency room were empty.

"Yeah, for sure." The discomfort had lessened. Luther shifted and tried to alleviate the pressure. "Why couldn't I see straight?"

"Viagra can decrease blood flow to the optic nerve. It can cause sudden vision loss. In your case, it appears your vision is almost back to normal. Since you aren't a regular user, it shouldn't cause any damage."

"So, the symptoms should just go away?"

"They should rather soon. I am interested in what's happening here, however." The doctor picked up Luther's hand and inspected his fingernails.

"Why?"

"I haven't seen this in a long, time. I want to take some blood tests just to explore and rule out possible causes."

"For what?"

"These lines across your nail beds. They're close to your cuticles. It suggests to me it's just been a few weeks or so. Have you had any major changes in your diet recently?"

"No. What is it, like iron deficiency?"

"It looks like, Mees' lines. See these horizontal, white bands on your nails?"

"Yeah, so?"

"Have you had any vomiting or diarrhea lately?"

"No vomiting but an upset stomach, dia—yeah, why?"

The doctor popped his head up, and he released Luther's hand. "Have you been sweating a lot?" He checked Luther's eyes and manhandled him as he examined him again. This time, his focus was far more serious.

"A little. I'm fighting off a bug or something, but I'm not worried about it. I've got a strong immune system."

"We'll just do a few more blood tests, and I'm sure it will be fine. Nothing to worry about, Mr. Evans."

"That's great. So, what's the treatment for this?" He folded his hands over his saluting soldier.

"Your erection should go away soon enough."

Luther could swear the doctor smirked as he turned away.

"So, what, there are no meds you can give me to make it stop?"

"No, sir, it's just going to need to run its course. The nurse will come back in a few moments to draw some more blood." The doctor exited the room. Muffled laughter came from out in the hallway, and Luther could have sworn his name was mentioned.

"Fantastic." He shook his head with frustration.

Jasmine sat quiet in the corner with her coat draped over her folded arms. She wore a spiteful frown, one he had never seen before.

"What's that look for? I already explained."

"Yes, you did, Luther. This is your most convincing one yet. Well, second most anyway."

"Second?"

"Yes, despite how sincere you act, this little stunt was the last straw." She stood and walked over to the hospital bed.

"Don't get all high and mighty on me."

"Worry not, dearest; you have no obligation to me anymore." She held her palm out then tossed the huge diamond ring in his lap.

"You're leaving me because of this?" He motioned to his groin.

"I'm leaving because you need the freedom of a single man, since you're living like one anyway, and all I want is someone who wants me. Only me."

"You're being dramatic again, Jazz."

"I am, huh?"

"Yes, you are."

"Maybe you should call your date back, then, because it doesn't seem like she got the memo about your engagement." Jasmine produced his cell phone, with an icy glower, and threw it on the bed beside him. "I'll be packed and gone before you get home. Whatever I can't take tonight, I'll send someone to pick up later."

Hatred fanned out from her piercing gawp. This rage was an expression he had ever seen on Jasmine's face before.

He sneered and flipped open his phone. The damning text message flashed at him. "What the f—?"

Baby, Justin's flight got canceled. Why don't you pop by again tonight and we'll pick up where we left off earlier. Maybe this time we can get you up to the challenge.

"That's just perfect." He shut the phone and tucked his chin to his chest.

"What? Did I interrupt your plans for the rest of the night? I mean, our well-intended friends are still at the house for what was supposed to be a surprise engagement party."

"Jazzy." He puckered his brows.

"What gets me the most is the crap you pulled to get me in the first place. And what was it all really for, another conquest? Do I mean that little to you?"

"What did I pull on you?" He looked at the floor in hopes she wouldn't find the truth in his eyes.

"The way you got Jason out of my life."

"Huh?" He met her vicious stare with his jaw agape.

"Did you honestly believe I was stupid enough I wouldn't have figured out you sent him away while you swooped in to win me over?"

"You knew the whole time?"

"Of course I did, you moron."

There is no way she could know everything. No one does.

"I got an urgent message to go to the front desk for a phone call. I walked all the way to the damn hotel. I knew when I got there and they had no idea what the hell I was talking about, you set it up. You had them send a fake message to get me away from him."

He pursed his lips and shook his head.

"Then, you got rid of him. When I finally walked all the way back to the cabana, he had left. He probably thought I baled on him. A mile, Luther, a whole friggin' mile to find myself stood up. And oh, how convenient you happened to stroll by with tickets for a boat cruise that night?"

"Jasmine, come on." He shrugged his shoulders.

"What I haven't figured out is what you said to keep him away. Did you bribe him? Huh? You know what, don't even bother. I don't want to know anymore."

"If you were so suspicious, why didn't you mention this before?"

"Because I've had it, Luther. I'm done."

Here it comes.

"You are the most—" She paced back and forth, her coat clutched in one arm, and flailed the other around as she ranted. "—arrogant, self-serving, manipulative, sadistic, uncaring, egocentric, chauvinistic, mean-spirited, egomaniacal, narcissistic...self-centered, greedy, reprehensible, vain, asshole I have ever met in my *entire* life." The veins in her temples pulsated.

"Shit, Jasmine, don't hold back. Why don't you say what's really on your mind." He lowered his gaze.

"I deserved better from you."

"Better?" He chortled.

"Hey!" she barked.

He glared up at her and waited for her head to spin around.

"Don't call me. Don't talk to me. Don't look for me. Don't even think about me. You don't ever contact me again. I hate you, you selfish bastard. I hope you rot in hell." She sobbed as she stormed out of the room.

"That went well." He picked up the huge ring and stared at it. The wind in his sails had officially diminished.

Chapter Four

TEXTING as he walked, Luther blinked hard to tried to see the screen. The damned Viagra—his vision was still fuzzy.

"Mr. Evans, can I call a cab for you?" He stopped and glanced over to find the cute nurse he flirted with earlier peek out from behind her station.

"Cab?" He glanced down at the incoming message. "No, thanks Ginny. I'll drive home." With his phone in one hand, he patted his pant pocket with the other to confirm Jasmine had left the keys to his BMW. "I'm good."

"The doctor suggested you shouldn't drive until the...."

He glanced at her again when she paused.

"Until the medication wears off." She eyed the front of his still-bulging pants, her heart-shaped face turning a pretty shade of crimson.

"Thanks, I'm fine." He trudged down the hall and forced his concrete-like feet, one in front of the other as he carried on down the corridor. *Sure, before I was dying to get laid and couldn't get it up. Here, I have a hard-on, and I have no interest in the hot nurse, or even going back to bang Jocelyn. Is this night ever gonna end?*

"Sooner than you think," a woman's whisper filled his ear.

Luther spun, but the hallway was empty. Great, he could add a little auditory hallucination to top the evening off. The phone buzzed in his hand again.

Sorry, buddy, Beth's home so you can't come here tonight. Jazz told her everything. She's pissed off. You should stay at the Plaza. Let me know when you get there, I'll pop over.

"Perfect," he grumbled.

No way would he go back to the house tonight, not while she packed to leave. He didn't want to deal with the aftermath. Getting out of pinches was his forte, not facing them.

To go to his father's was out of the question. Even if Jasmine hadn't already told him everything, the need to explain why he had to crash overnight held no appeal and no reprieve for Luther.

Marvin was right. The Plaza seemed like the only viable solution.

Sure, I'll head there. Should be a half hour or so. Gonna have a bite to eat and hit the sack. I'm wiped out. Luther finished the text then tucked his phone into his coat and took his keys out. He pressed the elevator button with a heavy sigh.

The clanking metal door dragged open with an irksome ding. Empty. At least he didn't have to paint on a smile. He inched into the grimy box and pressed *P5*. A bed was all he needed tonight, and no people to mingle with. The door scraped along the frame as it closed then got stuck only six inches before shutting.

"Gimme a break." He shoved his hand through to push it open. Immovable, the cold metal resisted. Anger flooded him, and he kicked the door while wrestling it back and forth, trying to get it to move. Without warning, the elevator door slammed shut. He yanked his hand back in the nick of time, saving his fingers from getting crushed. Luther's chest pounded, and a rush of sweat covered his forehead.

"That was close." A sharp jolt shook the elevator. Rattling sounded overhead, like a loose cable. The air grew thick. He couldn't breathe. *Am I about to meet my maker?* He snagged at the collar of his shirt then clicked the button again and again for the main floor, but the death trap door didn't budge. He stilled, terrified to shift in case something broke in the dilapidated wreck.

The quiet besieged him and rang in his ears. He waited, his pulse raced, his heartbeat thrummed behind his ears.

Luther sidestepped slowly to the console. He pushed the open button once again. It still didn't work. "I can't believe this," he hissed. Pins and needles filled his toes, traveling up his legs, followed by a prickling along his skin.

Desperation mounted and he pressed every button on the board, hoping something would free him. Then, a grinding sound, followed by the sudden plummeting, and his stomach bottomed out with the weightlessness.

No! The elevator plunged downward. Images flashed through his mind and words filled his head: *If you wrong another person, you will die.*

Is my nightmare crossing into reality?

With a frightful jerk, the elevator stopped and the door slid open. Stunned, he fixed his stare at the number *P5,* glowing above him. Luther bolted out of the elevator, and the door eased closed behind him with the tactless chime sounding again.

Speechless, even in his own mind, he fumbled with his keys and pressed the alarm button, triggering piercing chirps and flashing lights down at the end of the row. The commotion revealed his car in the sea of metal and wheels. Clicking the alarm off, he walked down the concrete path to the respite of his trusty BMW.

The sudden screech of tires ricocheted throughout the lot. It grew louder and closer as he walked the length of the parking garage. Luther spied the fast approaching car and jumped out of the path of the oncoming vehicle. The car full of teens sped away, with only the bass of blaring music sounding with rhythmic thuds, muffled by the closed windows.

Great. On top of the rest of the night, I'm paranoid, too. Weariness washed over him. He reached his silver car and climbed in.

CHAPTER FIVE

AS HE ducked into the lobby, he shook the rain off his coat and in a vain attempt, brushed at the residual moisture.

It's coming down like cats and dogs out there. He dragged his drenched feet as he headed to the front desk.

"Good evening, Jacques." He forced a smile at the mature concierge—one of the few people he hadn't managed to screw over or piss off.

"We had your usual suite prepped the moment you called. It's ready, Mr. Evans."

"Great. I need to dry off a little and get a good night's sleep." He lifted his cold, soaked shirt away from his chest with disgust. Luther pulled out his wallet and handed the concierge his gold card. "Uh, I didn't bring an overnight bag with me."

"I will have a bellhop carry up a robe and some pajamas from the gift shop for you, sir. We can send your clothing to the launderer to be ready for morning."

"Thanks. Add the cost to my card and give yourself a thirty percent tip."

"With pleasure, sir." Jacques handed back the plastic and a small cellophane sleeve with the room card in it.

Luther trudged across the corridor. Outside the vast lobby windows, the storm built momentum. Thunder rumbled long and deep. Lightning flashed. A bright radiance lit up the hotel lobby then darkened, reminding him of his little electrical incident, and he shuddered.

Pausing at the elevator, he stepped back, glanced over to the staircase door, and then looked back up to the numbers above the elevator.

The only other option would be to climb the stairs to the 26th floor. Overtaken by defeat, he shook his head and entered the open elevator and cringed. *I've had enough escapades for one night.*

Floor by excruciating floor, Luther focused on the numbers as he took shallow breaths and waited for the nerve-wracking ride to be done. The elevator operator smiled when Luther glimpsed to his side at him. *Maybe nothing will happen if someone else is in here with me.*

At long last they reached his floor, and Luther shimmied through the door before it was completely open.

The slide of the room key resounded a comforting beep. The familiar lair looked the same—elegant and hospitable, but with a certain emptiness. Any time he had come to stay, it was to rendezvous with clients so Jasmine wouldn't find out. Being alone in this hotel was a first for him. The absence of sneaking in with some hot chick left his enthusiasm to be here deficient.

Luther slid his drenched leather shoes off as he headed to the bed and flopped back onto the plush mattress like a lead weight. He closed his eyes and eased into a state of almost slumber.

A knock startled him, and he bolted up from the bed and answered the door.

"Room service, Mr. Evans."

Luther let the uniformed server enter. The gift shop bag he carried brought a welcome sight. A second man with a cart followed him in.

"Jacques took the liberty and sent up your favorite meal. There is also a beverage, as well as an envelope on the tray, addressed to you, sir."

"Who is it from?"

"I'm not sure, Mr. Evans. The champagne and envelope were left on the cart when I picked up your meal."

The lanky young lad unpackaged the robe and pajamas and laid them out on the bed while the heavyset, older man moved the trolley to the small dining table and arranged everything. He set linen, lit candles, and displayed cutlery and the meal on the small table.

"Roast chump of lamb rolled in herbs with petit ratatouille, gratin potatoes, and for dessert, rhubarb and champagne crème brûlée with crisp ginger short bread." The stocky man smiled and stood proud as he removed the silver domed lid.

The food didn't appeal, even though a sumptuous meal on any given day.

"Thank you, gentlemen." From his drenched jacket, he pulled out his wallet and presented them with a tip.

The older gentleman popped the cork on the champagne and poured it into a crystal flute, then placed the bottle in a bucket of ice. The cheery sound of the liquid as it hit the bottom of the glass was followed by the fizz of bubbles. The window lit up with sporadic flashes of light, and crashing thunder vibrated through the walls and glass.

They collected their gratuities with nods, excused themselves, then pushed the cart out of the room, pulling the door closed behind them.

Alone again, he glanced around the vacant room. The flickers of candlelight glistened against the glass and beckoned him. Luther picked up the small white envelope and read the note.

Sorry for your luck, buddy. Get some rest. The bubbly is on me.

Marvin.

A sigh escaped his lips as he dropped the paper on the table. Sudden thirst overtook him, and he collected the glass and inhaled the lemony bouquet. The first sip slowly rolled over his tongue, stingingly fresh and ethereal. Luther swallowed the effervescence; the rush of warmth and relaxation flowed through him. He emptied the glass in a few big gulps, and it tantalized his urge to drown his sorrows.

Ah, this is the good stuff. Eying the Dom Pérignon in the bucket. He picked it up and examined the label. A bottle of their finest might just help him settle in for a good night's sleep. Maybe by morning, this nightmare would be long gone. *Thanks, Marvin. A true friend.*

Luther set his empty glass on the table. He studied the clothing on the bed. The rain had soaked his current attire, which had grown cold and restrictive. The silver dome placed aside, he collected it and covered the piping hot meal as he decided to jump into the hot jet stream shower.

The steady torrent of blissful heat ran down his face and shoulders. The tension of his muscles remained constant, but the fragrant lather of lemon verbena refreshed his shattered soul. Hesitant to end his hot water asylum, he turned off the faucet and buried his face in the terrycloth towel, then dried off and stepped out of the shower. The cloud of steam enveloped the mirror and filled the air.

Refreshed, he slipped into the warm pj's then sat before the laid out dinner for a bite to eat. A second glass of delight began his meal and sparked his rant.

Deserved better, who is she kidding? She'll beg me to take her back by morning, I know it. He poured the next glass and basked in an alcohol-induced state of not giving a damn.

Jason was a broke-ass artist. He never could have given her half of what I did.

The events of the night filled his mind and evoked his frustration again as the warmth of the champagne trickled through his stomach.

He downed another one in a rush. The transcending froth encircled his mouth, and he filled the flute again.

I was good to her. I gave her everything she asked for. Pushing his chair back, he stormed over to his pile of clothes, fished through his pants pocket, retrieved the Tiffany engagement ring, and returned to his seat. Mesmerized by the glitter of the audacious bling, he shook his head with disbelief.

She knew I never wanted kids and accepted that. Dad doesn't know what the hell he's talking about.

The custom design of the thick platinum band and massive princess cut diamond made this bigger than any ring she had her eye on over the years they had been together.

Narcissistic? Greedy? Who the hell does she think she is? The anger seethed within him, his stomach stabbed with pain, and a sweat broke out over his face and body.

I'm better off single anyway. She just wanted my money, I know it. No one is that good, kind, and sweet. All an act. The bitterness consumed him, and the tingling in his hands and feet returned full force. In all his thirty-five years, he never let a woman get close enough to hurt him. He didn't intend to let her, yet here he sat, alone and miserable. All because of her.

How could I be such a blind idiot? She's not worth it. She never will be. Spouting his acrimony aloud didn't make any of his meaningless words true; it further magnified his self-pity.

The sparkle of the rock grew dim, and red flooded his vision. He dropped the ring into his glass of champagne in a moment of protest. Luther stood and held it up in front of him. Thunder boomed and lighting streaked across the sky outside his penthouse window as he yelled at the ceiling.

"For my so-called God, hear me. Never again. I'm looking after number one for the rest of my life. Screw everyone else and Jasmine." He sucked back the champagne with desperation, faster than he intended to. Divine numbness spread over his muscles.

A sharp pain filled his throat. He coughed and spewed the drink as he gasped for air. The crystal flute crashed to his dinner plate. Razor-like shards scattered across the table and down on the carpet as he gagged and choked. He tried to inhale, but he couldn't. The diamond ring was lodged in his throat.

Panic overtook him. He grabbed at his neck, and convulsed from lack of air. His limbs went numb. He fell to his knees. Everything faded around him, except a golden glow.

A gaseous cloud materialized. His strength waned. He dropped to the floor and braced himself from falling over. A man appeared in front him, like before, when he dreamt at night. A tall man with dark hair, dark eyes, and he had—wings? *What the hell is he doing here?* Willing his hands to lash out did nothing. His panic amplified as he knelt at the mercy of the figure.

"Fear not, Luther, I am here to help you." He took Luther's hand, helping him to his feet.

The pain in his throat vanished. He stopped choking. He drew in a long breath before he spoke. "Who are you?" Stunned, he examined the being, from head to toe. *Some elaborate outfit for room service.*

"I am, Azrael."

"A—Azr—this is so not funny." He shook his head and stepped back.

"Jeremiel warned of my arrival. There should be no surprise in my presence."

"Am I in the middle of another messed up dream?" Horror rushed through him, and he rubbed at his eyes. His vision was clear as day, unlike any dream he'd had before.

"You have crossed over, Luther." The glistening on his face snared Luther's attention.

"Are you—crying?"

"Yes."

"Why?"

"I weep for you."

"For me?" he growled. "Why would you cry for me?"

"Angels weep when we lose a human soul."

"What are you talking about?" Luther threw his hands up with irritation.

"I've been assigned to deliver you."

"Sure, where would that be? The post office?" He reeled back. *Eating before bed or downing too much alcohol? Whatever it is, I've gotta wake myself up.*

The winged apparition aimed a finger to the ground behind Luther. He turned around to see what he pointed at.

"To purgatory."

There, on the floor where he had choked, was—him. His face and lips had turned blue; his eyes bulged and were wide open. He patted himself up and down.

Holy crap, is that my body on the ground? Luther knelt and poked at the body with his finger. When his finger disappeared into the body, a jolt of terror shot through him.

"You are a spirit, in ethereal form. You're not able to touch solid matter in this state."

Luther scrambled to his feet and gasped. *It can't be. Can it?* He slapped himself. Nothing changed. *Am I dead? This can't be real. What the fuck?*

"This is not a dream. You were forewarned, you made a conscious choice, and it's time to pay the price."

"Price for what?"

"Harming others, for greed, for being self-serving at the expense of the one who loved you."

"Jasmine?"

"It's time." The Angel of Death held his hand out, but Luther resisted.

"I'm not going anywhere with you."

Chapter Six

"WHERE are we?" He gritted his teeth and snarled.

The Archangel of Death didn't say a word but remained on route to a tall white structure.

"Look, I'm not interested in the grand tour." As Luther eyed the large Parthenon-styled building, the weighted fear in his chest tightened. "Hey, I'm talking to you."

"My name is Azrael."

"Yeah, I got that. Listen, I'm only thirty-five. In perfect health and the prime of my life."

"Perhaps you were."

At the foot of the long slate-stoned lane to the massive edifice, Azrael motioned with his hand for Luther to follow the path to the entrance.

"We are at the Great Hall."

"What's in the—? Wait a minute, I know this place." An onslaught of memories saturated his mind, of his childhood, when he sat at the desk, studied the bible and listened as his father prepared sermons each week.

"The Akashic Records."

"Isn't that like the story of my life?"

"It is the records of all life, the master blueprint for the universe, so to speak."

"This is bad, isn't it?" Luther clamped his hands over his face and heaved a sigh.

"I see you do recall some of your religious education?"

"It's impossible not to. I've had daily lessons and lectures for fifteen years. It's unavoidable."

"Come, Metatron awaits your arrival."

Frozen with fear, Luther didn't move an inch. "Metatron? I remember the story...."

"Go on."

"He was one of the only two archangels whose name didn't end in "el" and...." He squinted, and searched his faint memory for the rest. A trivial thing to remember given the circumstances but a start. Then he glanced up at his winged adversary. "One of the only two who were humans before becoming angels. He and his brother, Elijah—Sandalphon."

"Correct. He went by Enoch as a human."

Luther nodded.

"On Earth, Enoch served as a prophet and scribe but was also a scholar on heavenly secrets. As a result, God escorted Enoch directly to the Seventh Heaven—the highest level—to reside and work." The creature stood tall and spoke with a stern voice.

"I remember some of this."

"God gave Enoch wings and transformed him into an archangel. Since Metatron excelled at his work on Earth, he holds a similar job in Heaven, to scribe everything that happens on Earth and keep the Akashic records, otherwise known as the *Book of Life*. He is the keeper in charge and helps humans understand Heaven's perspective, teaching newcomers how to work with the angelic realm."

"If I have to go to Purgatory, why are we here?"

"To meet with Jeremiel and Metatron. To be fair, a review of the records of your life will be completed before the sentence is handed down."

"You mean it's not a done deal yet?" Hope sprouted.

"Eternal damnation you have earned, but the punishment must fit the crime. To determine your penance, they will review your human existence and then decide."

"They? Where are you going?"

"My responsibility is to help you cross over and to deliver you here. There are others that await my arrival."

"Lucky them." Luther turned with a cringe as he faced the hall. As he neared the door, he sucked in a breath and tried to work up the courage to face his prosecutors.

"Hey—" He glanced over his shoulder, but Azrael had vanished.

Each step he took made it more real for him, scarier. The lingering doom amplified. Hesitant, he eyed the ornate, gold door handle and pushed his fingers through his hair, doing his best to work up the nerve.

Better to just get it over with. Like ripping a Band-Aid off...of my scrotum. Ready to enter, he reached for the handle, but the door opened without his touch.

Cautious, Luther stepped over the marble threshold and scouted around the colossal hall. The sounds of his steps echoed. The walls were filled with massive shelves that spanned all the way to the ceiling, housing thousands of bound books. The floor appeared bare, everything shone with a remarkable brightness, despite how it had become the darkest day he had ever experienced.

"Welcome, Luther. Please join us," a deep voice echoed. He followed the sound and spotted a table with two men, or rather angels, who sat behind it and faced him. One looked familiar, the other must be Metatron.

"Oh, it's you." He eyed Jeremiel with defiance. "I remember you. You're the one who likes to shake beds and —did you electrocute me?"

"Sit down." He motioned to a third chair on the opposing side of the table.

Compliant, he dropped into the seat and faced his judge and jury.

"You've been a busy man, Luther." Metatron opened a monstrous book and gazed at the pages that appeared to flip themselves.

Don't say a word. This is the time to keep my mouth shut. Maybe I can get out of this.

"Gabrielle, you should be present to hear the logistics of your charge's case." Metatron lifted his head as he called out.

A vapor appeared beside him and then erupted into a quick flash of flame. In its wake stood a magnificent creature, another angel, a woman who shimmered with regal beauty. She remained silent, but her presence was undeniable.

The sheen of her hair held the rich copper tones of the sunset and trailed down her back. An azure blue cloak draped her body, and underneath she wore what he could only describe as an iridescent bodysuit with an intricate silhouette of an Eagle fused in silver across her breastplate. In her hand glimmered a gold chalice, encrusted in jewels.

"Her charge?" were the mere words he could spit out, in awe of her beauty.

"Metatron, must I accept this responsibility? It seems a vain attempt at redemption." The lunar blue of her eyes glowed, while she shot a fiery glare at Luther. Her lips pressed tight. "Gabrielle, you have your orders."

"Yes, but as I watched over him, I saw no reason for hope."

"You were watching me?" A sharp sense of violation rushed through him.

"It is not for you to judge a charge. It is for you to guide him."

"As you wish." She nodded, and the record keeper's gaze returned to the book in front of him.

"What's going on here?" Finding it hard to keep his eyes off her, Luther looked back to the two angels that sat at the table as they reviewed the events of his life.

Another angel appeared.

"Who are you?"

"I am the Archangel, Chamuel."

"So, I've already met Azrael, the executioner, what are you gonna do to me?"

"Luther, Chamuel is here to help. Bind your tongue and listen." The magnificent female spoke in a firm tone.

"Help?" He scoffed.

"My role is to heal the bonds of love. If you're unable to feel love, if your heart has hardened because you have lost someone close through death or separation, I—"

"I don't love because I don't need to." He sneered and turned his back.

"You do need to. More than ever before. You loved so much once, you *felt like you could fly*." The newest winged nightmare spoke with a gentle tone.

He spun around with his mouth open and eyes wide.

"Those were the last words you said to your mother," the angel continued.

Tongue-tied for a moment, he glared at Chamuel with bitterness. "Leave her out of this."

"Perhaps I didn't spend enough time with you when your mother crossed over. You were such a sad and angry boy."

"You guys have all the answers. Why are we discussing this?" Their intrusion grated on his nerves.

"Luther, once, a long time ago, you were a kind-hearted boy. You had so much love and generosity for others. Then, you changed and became a predator, who set out to sabotage the lives of many, serving your own needs at the expense of those who loved you the most." Metatron stared him down as he scolded him.

"Sounds like you've already decided my fate."

"If there is one who can speak for the kindness you once held in your heart, the compassion you had but cast away, we will consider a chance at redemption." Jeremiel's voice sounded softer than his counterpart.

"Okay, it seems to be crowded in here already. Is there another angel around here I can't see?" He glanced all over the massive hall with a one-sided smirk, cynical at the suggestion he would have an advocate in this place, his own personal hell.

"An angel perhaps, but not an archangel." The blue-eyed beauty lifted her chin as she spoke.

"Oh, and who would that be?" To contain his amusement would be easy, but his fear overruled it.

"Gladys, we require your presence," she called out.

"Luther, my darling." The sweetest voice sang out behind him, and he swung around to find his lifelong dream standing in front of him.

"Mom?" His chin quivered, disbelief inundating his heart.

"How I've missed you, son." She held her arms open, her smile lighting up her hazel green eyes.

"This is a bad joke. Ha ha, very funny." He reeled back and tried to contain the pricking tears.

"This is no joke. This is your last chance to save your soul," the brash voice sounded from behind the book.

Luther looked to his mother, astounded she stood right in front of his very eyes. If he hadn't renounced God when she died, he would have prayed for this a long time ago.

In the same way she did in his youth, Gladys stepped in and collected him in her embrace. The memorable lavender fragrance he cherished so long ago swathed him.

"Mom?" Weepiness filled him, and he hugged her back, not willing to let go.

"For the sake of my son, I beg of you. Please give him one last chance to make things right." She held him tight. "He is a good person. My death broke his heart. I thought he would have been resilient enough to accept God's love to heal."

"Gladys, you and your husband both have been the epitome of benevolence in living your humanity. For you and your service to God, Luther will be given one opportunity for deliverance. However, if he fails, spiritual exile will be his fate."

"Thank you." The whisper of her voice shrouded him with such love. The peace her simple touch gave him, he'd missed for so long.

"It's time for me to go, son." She released her embrace and faced him with glistening eyes.

"What? No, you can't leave, not again." A burst of grief surged through his chest, and he clung to her.

Gladys cupped his face in her palms, then leaned in, kissed his forehead, and drew back as she studied him. "You have work to do, my son. If you manage to do what they ask of you, we can be together again, here in Heaven. I know I can count on you to do the right thing. I've watched you over the years, and some of your choices have saddened me. You did things I never imagined you capable of. It's time to right the wrongs you've done. You have a great deal to undo."

Luther fixed his gaze on the ground, avoiding her stare. He clenched his teeth and held back a sob. "You saw, you knew?"

"Everything."

His heart sank. He had been wrong all this time. He had more than one external conscience. If he even had a clue his mother could see, he would have been a very diffcrent man when he'd lived.

"I love you, Luther. Peace be with you. It will be a difficult journey at best, but I know you can get through this. Find the strength in your heart, and you will find me there, too."

A single tear spilled down his cheek and then, she disappeared. Luther swallowed hard and flexed his jaw as he tried to gather his strength. "That was a dirty trick." How he hated them for it.

"Your chance to correct your misdeeds begins at this very moment." Metatron's harsh voice roused him from his lulled state, and he turned around to face him.

"You have a list of specific tasks to complete." Metatron nodded to the woman at his side.

"What tasks?"

The angelic goddess held out her empty hand, and a golden scroll materialized in it.

"Gabrielle will guide you through your assignment," the persecutor continued.

"Her?" Intrigue surfaced.

"She will also ensure you adhere to the rules."

"What rules?"

"To acquire salvation is no easy feat. There is a long list of people you have caused harm and pain to over the years."

"This is a joke, right? I could spend a whole lifetime trying to make up for every single one of them."

"True as that may be, one of your stipulations is you have seven days to complete this assignment."

"Seven days? How am I supposed to—?"

Luther looked to Gabrielle who shook her head side-to-side with furrowed brows; she made a hushing gesture with her lips and then faced her superior.

"In order to tend to the matters at hand, you will return to the mortal realm in human form. Not that of who you were, but a human, nonetheless." Jeremiel spoke in a less punitive tone.

"Your responsibilities will be as follows." Metatron's amber eyes glowed. His stern voice loud and commanding.

"Task number one: you must witness authentic truth. Number two: you must fully experience empathy. Three: you must demonstrate compassion, and the forth task is that you must learn the value of self-sacrifice."

"Is that all?" he scoffed.

"There is one more thing," Gabrielle chimed in. She held her radiant chalice up.

"What's that?" *Saving the best till last? This must be a doosie.*

"Your fifth and final assignment is that you must experience unconditional love, in its purest form."

"That sounds easy enough, in seven days, in human form. Is there anything else I need to know about? Am I supposed to end world hunger while I'm at it?"

Cringing at his own stupidity, he bit his lip as he watched Metatron and waited for his response. Luther expected a proverbial bomb to drop at this point. *That's it, be a smartass. That should help you plead your case.*

"No one is to know who you are or why you are there."

This angel must be incapable of any other expression.

"You are to seek no personal gratification, whatsoever." Jeremiel's expression shifted and matched his co-conspirator. "You cannot acquire recognition for any deeds completed. All has to be done in secret, in a pay it forward manner."

"I am to ensure you complete every item on this list." The luminescent blue of Gabrielle's eyes didn't soften the play-by-play.

"I know there's one more left, so give it to me." Like waiting for a punch in the gut, he stood, prepared for the worst.

"Three strikes and you are out." Metatron's guise altered. If Luther didn't know any better, he could have sworn the winged masochist was being smug.

"Meaning?"

"You have your tasks, your rules, and you will not have any second chances. Any rule you break, you get a strike. If you obtain three strikes, then you fail, and your sentence will be purgatory for all eternity."

"What if I am successful, then what happens to me?"

"We will not review any other options unless this assignment is completed."

"Whatever happened to innocent until proven guilty?"

The three-way glowers shot in his direction suggested none of the archangels had a sense of humor.

"Nothing like giving a guy something to look forward to."

Chapter Seven

"SO, WHAT'S with the cup?" The effort to make small talk proved a huge feat.

"This is the Chalice of Love; however, we have no need for this in your case." She gave him a stern glare, held the cup up, and it vanished in a poof.

"Nice." He shook his head with dismay.

"I didn't create this situation. I'm here to see it through."

"Why are we here? This is my dad's church." As he stood at her side, he looked to the closed door of the chapel, hesitant to enter. Cars filled the parking lot, and the black hearse at the side door gave him the chills. The rainy day didn't help. Back in human form again, the dampness and the cold chilled him to the bone.

"Your first commission is to witness authentic truth."

Luther faced Gabrielle again, to find her in a sleek, form-fitting black suit with a white blouse and high heels.

"Wow! What's with the digs?"

"These old things?" Gabrielle smirked and rolled open the golden scroll in her very elaborate getup. In fact, her appearance could distract him from his mission; after all, wouldn't it be blasphemy to have the hots for an archangel?

"Where are your wings?"

"I'm incognito, although no one else will see me, unless I decide it is necessary."

"So, is this the list?"

The corners of her mouth pulled back into a mischievous grin. In her hand, the scroll morphed into an iPhone. "Here, you can follow your list with this."

"They have an App for that?" He raised his brows and inspected it before she took it back.

"Sure they do. For every item on there, once it is complete, the phone will ring and the item will be crossed off. A self-monitoring checklist, so-to-speak. This way, you can keep track. Your first task begins in there." She motioned to the door with her hand and it opened.

"How long is this cryptic communication gonna go on?" He waited for a reply to his smartass question, but got none. That is, except when she prompted him with her gaze, toward the door of the church. He glanced down to find his own attire changed to a black suit with a black dress shirt and a beige tie.

Three quarters of the chapel were filled, most by older people, friends and parishioners of his father's from over the years. At the front of the church, he fixed his sight on the wooden casket, draped with red roses, white lilies and carnations. Beside it stood a tall easel with a large photograph of the deceased—him?

"You brought me to attend my own funeral? Isn't that kind of a Scrooge cliché?" Luther turned around and Gabrielle had vanished.

"Great," he huffed.

"Shhhh." He couldn't tell who had hushed him but proceeded in silence down the aisle as he tried not to draw any further attention.

The back third section of pews was sparsely populated with people all dressed in black. So, he spotted a seat where he would be unobtrusive and sat down on the squeaky, hard wood. The church remained quiet, except for the occasional echoed cough or two and a small child near the front, who fussed and cried.

The bountiful display of sympathy floral arrangements caught his eye. It had never occurred to him to imagine who would attend his funeral or even what it would be like. True to form, it appeared his dad had everything arranged to perfection.

My dad? Where is he? The one person, who would have been crushed by his death, would be his father.

"I can't help but think about Pastor Evans, that poor man." A woman a few rows in front of Luther whispered in a somewhat curt tone. "The horrible things his son did. How could such a gentle, kind man raise a beast like that for a son?"

Well, that was rude. He didn't recognize the middle-aged woman. She continued to chat to her neighbor on the bench, loud enough that others turned back. An older woman a few rows up glowered at the chatty lady. She placed her finger to her pursed lips and gave an abrupt "shush". The gossip paused until the woman turned around, and then she started again.

"Did you know what he did to Sandra Foley?"

You must be one of the know-it-alls who fed Dad the local gossip. Luther had enough of the hag. He got up and went to another pew on the other side of the church. In front of him, a row of women sat, dressed in dark clothes, some wearing little hats with veils. One sobbed and held a handkerchief to her face. He admired her off the shoulders, sexy black dress and wild curls, and then recognized the mass of platinum locks.

Jocelyn. With a smile of relief, he watched the back of her head shake from side-to-side as she sniffled and shuddered when she inhaled. At least he had one fan in the audience. Beside her, an older, graying man sat. It must have been Justin, her husband.

"I'm glad the thieving bastard is dead. If he hadn't croaked, I would've killed him myself," he whispered in a gruff voice into her ear. "Quit your sniveling."

"Darling, please," Jocelyn begged.

"I know all about his conniving ways. There are at least ten women in this room alone he screwed over. Half of them are in divorce court. Count your lucky stars you aren't one of them."

"You know I love you, baby. I never meant—"

"Look, I already told you, I saw the house security videos. You're lucky I didn't throw you out on your damn ass that night."

"We didn't do anything. I'm sorry."

Ouch. I guess he knew what we were up to after all.

Enough of the dynamic duo for him, Luther inched his way down to the other end of the pew. Luther hoped this seat proved to be far enough away he didn't have to listen to any more critiques from the congregation.

"Excuse me, please." A woman in a short, black dress with chiffon sleeves coaxed him to allow her access. He moved his knees to the side, and she eased past him to the middle of the pew to sit down.

The side door to the alter area opened, and in walked Jasper, leaning heavy on his cane. Luther studied the red, blotchy spots over his dad's forehead, his swollen, puffy eyes and rims. He gathered his father must have cried before he came out.

He stood at the podium, cleared his throat, and began his speech.

"Thank you all for joining us here, at this most difficult time. Three days ago, our worlds were forever changed by tragedy." His voice quaked. He didn't sound at all like the strong, virile man his father had always been. His dad seemed so fragile and listless.

"Today, we gather to celebrate the life of Luther Evans, taken too soon." His dad's chin quivered as he choked up and reached over to touch the casket.

"Many of you knew my son and know the undying love I had for him...." At the sight of his father's grief, Luther's chest tightened and tears pricked at his eyes. He never wanted him to be left alone. As fate would have it, Jasper was.

Luther remained focused on his father, struggling to hear his words with his softened voice and the shifting of people in their seats. His new bench mate sat quiet and still. He looked over and spotted her black, floppy wide brim hat with birdcage lace that covered her face. Then, walloping surprise shot through him. His jaw agape, he fought the urge to call out to her. *Jasmine.*

Another glimpse. Luther was shocked to see the much-feared Angel of death sitting at Jasmine's side.

Gabrielle, he's not gonna kill her is he? A panicked whisper slipped out.

No, it is not her time to die.
Why is he with Jasmine?

"Sssshhhh," an irritated whisper sounded behind him.

It is his task to counsel her through your passing.

But he's the Angel of Death, right?

Azrael has many duties. Helping those cross over from their physical deaths is simply one of them. He also counsels those in mourning to help them through the difficult time.

It hadn't occurred to Luther, in his bout of self-pity and panic for his soul, that others might be impacted by his death.

Although dead for such a short time, it amazed Luther how quickly he'd forgotten Jasmine's exquisite beauty. At first glance all those years ago in Mexico, and again at this moment, he admired the perfect structure of her high cheekbones, her long raven hair, full ruby lips, and ice blue eyes. She wore an uncharacteristic blank expression on her face, almost void, like on the night of their surprise party when he got angry with her. There were no signs of distress. Her makeup proved flawless. There weren't even any tears. Beside Jasmine was the petite brunette who had watched over his father since his mother died. The maid, Sarah, dabbed away tears with a handkerchief. Despite the formality of her role in the home, she had always been so kind and supportive of his father. Never one of Luther's fans, regardless, Sarah had always been polite.

How come Jasmine isn't upset? I know she loved me. I thought her and Dad would have at least been sad.

Gabrielle materialized in the seat beside him. "Her heart has hardened because of you. She can't even allow herself to mourn your death. She is hurt and angry."

"Thanks for the play-by-play," he offered with a hushed voice.

"Ssshhh." The person in the rows up ahead turned around and fired a menacing glare.

"Sorry," he mouthed and tucked his chin down.

Can she recognize me?

No. Gabrielle pointed to a reflective surface on a large framed canvas on the wall next to him. There, he saw a blonde man with hazel green eyes, who in no way resembled him.

To remain for the entire service had been a torment he had to endure. Standing at his own graveside, there were no words to describe the surreal sensation of doom and finality. As he scanned the gathered crowd, it occurred to him not everyone from the church attended the burial. In fact, there must have been maybe twenty people or so in total, a far cry from the near full congregation. Jasper persisted in his deliverance of an eloquent service, despite the snide remarks the occasional ex-clients made. His father continued as if he hadn't heard a single word of negativity.

Jasmine stood at Jasper's side and held his hand as her vacant stare remained fixed on the hole in the ground. Still, she showed not one ounce of emotion.

She and Dad have grown close and very fond of one another over the last five years.

What choice did they have, you were never available to either one of them emotionally.

Thank you for that—helpful—observation.

My pleasure. Gabrielle stood to the left of him, commentating on every thought he had.

"Do you mind?" he grumbled out loud. Everyone looked at him, and his cheeks burned. "Sorry, please, go on."

One absent face he discovered belonged to his long-time friend, Marvin. Surprised at his non-appearance, the six ladies that stood side-by-side and held hands snagged his attention.

Upon closer look, each of them appeared familiar. All past clients, all conquests for sex and money. Each lady wore black attire with a veil, each had a red rose pinned on their lapel, and each wore—red stiletto heels?

They all agreed to dance on your grave, in red, after you were buried.

Nice, thanks a lot.

You're welcome. An impish smirk lit up her iridescent face.

You're getting far too much pleasure from my death, aren't you?

When one considers the amount of work you have caused me over the years, perhaps I am overindulging a little.

Work? What for?

Like all the other archangels, I have many purposes, Luther. I help those who find themselves at a loss, those who need to find their path. I also assist women who have been raped or sexually assaulted and feel violated.

Hey, easy there princess, I never raped or sexually assaulted anyone in my entire life.

Perhaps not with force, but Luther, can you not see the aftermath of the people you took advantage of? It's psychological rape. They trusted who you professed to be, with your promises of grandeur, only to be left reeling from loss of money, possessions, and relationships. Once you took what you wanted, you discarded them like garbage and left them to fend for themselves after they lost everything.

That's a little over dramatic.

Really?

Speechless, he had no words left to banter back. Skepticism consumed him at the thought of having this kind of impact on people.

Some guide you've turned out to be.

You never stuck around long enough to know any different.

I get it, okay. Can you just please shut up for a minute?

His jaw clenched tight as he remembered not to bark his annoyance out loud again. No one else could see and hear his tormentor.

Overwhelmed, the urge to stand closer to Jasper and Jasmine encased him. With tactful side steps, he inched his way nearer to them. He wanted so much to reach out to his dad. Azrael stood between them both, with a neutral expression. The mere sight of him infuriated Luther.

The thumping of his heart grew slow and forceful. His chest began to hurt, and pressure built in his forehead. A stuffy sensation in his sinuses developed.

What is this in my chest and head? Am I dying again?

On the contrary, Luther, in order for you to understand and learn compassion, you have been gifted with a potent empathic ability.

Meaning? He rubbed his chest.

You have the divine privilege of feeling the pain and suffering of those physically close to you. She nodded at Jasper. *Your current experience is the corporeal symptoms of your father's excessive grief.*

Dad? Shame filled his aching heart as he massaged it and looked at his father's pale, brave exterior.

What about Jasmine? Is she in the same kind of pain?

You can sense for yourself. Close your eyes and focus. See in your mind's eye into her heart and allow yourself to feel her emotions.

Hesitant, his curiosity beat out his sense of avoidance. He did as she told him and tried for what seemed a long time.

It's not working. I can't feel her.

On the contrary, Luther. That is exactly what she is feeling. No reaction.

Is she in shock?

Jasmine has been in pain over you for so long, your death pushed her over the edge to numbness.

Jazzy. He gripped his lapel and resisted the urge to reach out to her.

Come, it's time to move on. Gabrielle pulled out her iPhone and investigated the screen.

To where?

In a vain attempt to get a glimpse, he leaned nearer to the angel to see, and she sharply moved away. Another step closer to get a peek of the phone and he lost his balance.

Chapter Eight

ENTERING the hotel suite, he tripped over the threshold.

"Watch your step, Luther."

"Very funny. You knew I would fall into my own grave and did that on purpose, didn't you?"

"Perhaps you're paranoid? It's not like I electrocuted you." She held her fingernails up and inspected them with a smug smile. "Or blew up a lighter in your face, or dropped an elevator."

Shock flushed through him. "You did that?"

Gabrielle winked.

"You're an angel. How could you?"

"Call it the angel's *Karma* card. There has to be some perks to this job, after cleaning up all the messes you have made over the years, the affliction you caused, the—"

"Yeah, yeah, I get it, no need to explain further." Luther sat on the edge of the mattress, dropped his head into his hands, and sighed.

"It's a lot to endure in the first day, isn't it?" Gabrielle tossed the iPhone into his lap, sat in the armchair, and faced him.

"Is that sympathy I hear?" When Luther glanced up, he found her gentle smile.

"You caught me at a moment of weakness. Don't worry, it won't happen again." She lifted her chin with her eyes still aglow, sat back into her chair, crossed one leg over the other, and dangled her foot.

"Wonderful." He flopped back onto the bed. Exhaustion overtook him, and he didn't have the strength to fight.

***

BRIGHTNESS permeated his closed lids, and he buried his face into the pillow. "Jasmine, turn the damn light off."

"Charming." A feminine voice roused him.

He bolted up in the bed, to find Gabrielle in the same chair, watching him. "What? Oh, right, you. I hoped this was all a crazy dream."

"No such luck, sunshine. Up and at `em, you're burning sunlight, and it's already day two."

"Day two? Why the hell did you let me fall asleep?"

"You are in a human body, Luther. You have the same physical needs. Food, water, sleep."

He caught her raising one brow as she glanced below his stomach.

"Those aren't the only needs." He leaned sideways and pulled the blanket over his lap.

"Yes, and as unfortunate at it may be, that is one need you'll have to live without. No self-gratification on your assignment." She mocked him with an insincere pout.

"Thanks for the recap," he snarled. "Could you...I don't know, turn around or do something useful like get me breakfast?" His effort to hide his arousal was an awkward task.

"I'm here to guide, not to serve. Get your own breakfast." Gabrielle vanished.

"Just peachy."

***

"SO, WHERE are we off to?" As they walked through the lobby, Luther eyed the gray-haired concierge and turned his head away when they passed.

"He won't recognize you. No one will."

"Right. Where to?"

"Check your phone, Einstein. Honestly, how you became a Wall Street hotshot with your lack of brainpower or retention is beyond me."

Luther sneered at her, but it brought no relief to his agitation. He pulled the smart phone out of his pocket and tapped the screen.

Witness authentic truth: Attend Jasper Evans's home, in spirit only.

"What is this supposed to mean? I went to my funeral. I heard some pretty crappy honesty. Can't we move on to the next task?"

"It means, some of the truth you need to hear will be shared in private." Gabrielle took his hand in hers.

"We're holding hands now?" He grinned.

"For a purpose. Lose the arrogance. It's very unattractive."

In a flash, they stood in his father's den. Jasper and Jasmine sat in the wing-backed chairs, facing one another. Both appeared frail, their eyes seemed heavy.

"Can they hear me?"

"No. You don't need to whisper here."

"What's up? They're still grieving me, aren't they?" Convinced he read the situation accurately, he offered more opinion than curiosity.

"Sssshhhhh."

"Jasper, I don't understand how this could have happened. I know Luther had his financial affairs in order. He had everything finalized," Jasmine sobbed.

"See, I knew she was after my money." Luther crossed his arms and pursed his lips.

The sharp elbow Gabrielle jabbed into his ribs hurt like hell.

"What did you do that for?"

"Close your mouth and listen." She narrowed her eyes and unleashed the lunar glow of her annoyance.

"From what I've read in the eviction notice here, he left assets to Marvin, who he also named as executor." Jasper read the paper in his hands aloud. "I'll have my lawyer investigate this, but as it stands, it doesn't look good for us I'm afraid."

"Marvin? What the f—?" He lunged forward, and Gabrielle grabbed his arm.

"If you don't shut your mouth and pay attention...." She held up her hand and a roll of duct tape materialized. "I will tape it up."

Silent, Luther dipped his head down and focused again.

"Luther told me he had all his paperwork completed and Marvin was supposed to get it notarized. He never said he'd made Marvin the legal representative." Jasper crunched the papers in his hand. His father gritted his teeth behind his grimace.

"Is there any way to challenge it, Jasper? He took the house, the cars, all his bank accounts, his bonds, everything. Luther named you his sole beneficiary. He told me so." Jasmine sniffed back her tears.

"I don't see how we can dispute this, Jasmine. I'm so sorry."

"Please don't apologize, you haven't done anything wrong. You've been like a father to me since I met him. I can take care of myself; I still work at the gallery. In fact, what I'm worried about is you. Where will you go?"

"Go?" Luther looked around the room in more detail and noticed some boxes, half packed in the corner. Shock consumed him, and he wandered around his father's home, where he found more items in crates, strewn about. The portrait of his mother in the dining room had been taken down and sat on the floor against the wall.

"Gabrielle, I don't understand. What's is all this?" He rushed back to the room and stood beside Jasper.

"When your father found out about the women you had scammed, he replaced the money you took with his own."

"What?" Anger flashed through him.

"You can imagine, over the past five years, dozens of women, millions of dollars. Your father is broke."

"That's not possible."

"Jasper Evans is a model of kindness and generosity. The thought of others in financial distress at your hands drowned him with guilt. He tried to make up for all the bad you had done."

"The house had already been paid for, and I left him everything I had. Why is he moving?"

"Marvin managed to have the deed to your parents' home put into your name. Therefore, when you died, he took that, too. He's evicted both of them."

"How could he do this? I never named him power of attorney or left him anything."

"Perhaps not, but that didn't stop him, did it?"

"But, I trusted him. Why would he do this?"

"Luther, for a cunning thief, I'm surprised you are so naïve. A man who earned his fortune, bilking millions of dollars from innocent clients through scams, the one person you trusted with your own financial affairs was the person who helped you rip off every single person."

His heart pounded, his breathing sped up. "It can't be true."

"I'll be fine, Jasmine. I have a little left I can get by on. The only thing I want, I need, is the portrait of my Gladys. As long as she is still with me, I can get through anything."

"Dad." A fierce ache penetrated Luther's chest. It wasn't his own heartbreak that hurt so much, but rather his father's and Jasmine's. He rubbed his sternum and shook his head.

"Hmmm, your empathic ability is operational, I see." Gabrielle nodded at the proximity of Luther to his loved ones.

"Jasmine, I want you to stay with me. We can find a small place with three bedrooms. You can't continue to work."

Her lip quivered. "Jasper, that's very sweet of you, but I don't want to be a burden."

"You're family, and I don't want you to be alone through this. At least we'll still have a part of Luther with us."

"What's he talking about?" He glanced back and forth between them as he studied their half-wide smiles through tears, and then to Gabrielle. With raised brows, he shrugged his shoulders. "I don't understand what they mean."

"Listen," she growled.

"I didn't plan to keep it. I knew how he felt about... this, but...."

"Keep what?" he grumbled and examined Jasmine's face. An expression of joy he hadn't seen in a long time emerged, and her eyes lit up.

Looking back to Jasper, his smile brightened his eyes, too. He followed the direction of his father's gaze and found —Jasmine, caressing her stomach.

"What?"

Chapter Nine

STILL shell-shocked, he sat on the bench and looked out at the Manhattan Waterfront Greenway.

"You haven't checked your phone yet. Can't you hear the sound in your pocket?" Gabrielle stood at the barrier of the water and faced him.

"My phone?" He rubbed his eyes and tried to brush away the moisture of his astonishment. Reaching into his coat pocket, he pulled out the cell phone and touched the screen. The cheerful chimes stopped, and the green words, *First task completed,* glowed.

"Great, now what?" He stared at the slender rectangle. *Task number two: You must fully experience empathy.*

"Well, didn't I already finish this little diddy?" The words that left his mouth fell flat, and he rubbed the residual pain in his chest.

"If you did, it would have rang and said completed."

"I just got screwed over royally by my best friend—the one person I trusted. I got a taste of my own medicine, so I know how it feels. Done." Luther stood up, his frustration streamed full force. Tempted to fling the phone into the Hudson River, he clenched it tight, walked back to the fence beside her, and leaned on the rail. He stared at the water, his disturbance consumed him.

"Luther, empathy is more than experiencing the same unhappiness another has felt."

"I don't see how. It's about understanding. I get it. Can we move on?"

"For you to debate the rules will not help you."

"Fine, empathy. Where next, chief?" he snapped.

"That, you will have to figure out on your own. I have business to tend to."

"What?"

Gabrielle vanished.

"Are you kidding me?" He threw his hands up to the sky and growled.

He had no clue where to go or what to do next. Luther started down the path. In the distance he could see the white bridge of the Northern Harlem Speedway. The sun shone hot in the clear blue sky. Flickers of light glimmered off windshields of the vehicles that passed by in early afternoon. The weight of his jacket grew constrictive. He flung it off and gripped it in his tense hand, continuing down the path.

The quiet all around seemed unusual for Manhattan. The green park was clean but very empty for the middle of the day. No bikers, roller bladders, or walkers. Just him and the cars that passed by over the bridge.

A baby? She's gonna have my baby? Unbelievable. And Marvin, what the hell was that about? I'm gonna find that little shit and kick the crap out of him. That thief. That devious bastard.

The violation that overtook him brought back Gabrielle's words at his graveside.

Luther, can you not see the aftermath of taking advantage of people? It's like psychological rape. They trusted you.... Once you took what you wanted, you left them to fend for themselves after they lost everything.

A surge of ache filled his head, and he rubbed his temples.

The sudden screech of tires startled him; he followed the squeals and looked up to the bridge. A car horn honked, long and shrill, more tires grabbed pavement and then a huge smashing sound resonated throughout the air of the waterway. Next, a black car plummeted over the bridge and crashed at the water's edge.

"Holy shit." He raced up to the car, but no one was around to help. The vehicle had landed upside down. Black smoke spewed from the engine and the tires spun. The motor stopped on impact. Unsure of what to do, Luther approached the driver's side, and bent down to investigate inside the shattered window. Dangling upside down, he found a single man, trapped, held up by a seatbelt. The middle-aged man had fallen unconscious, and blood seeped down his face.

"Hang on, buddy. I'll get some help." He reached for his phone to call 911. The screen read *OUT OF SERVICE.*

"Ah, come on. Gimme a break." He tossed the phone aside, stepped back, and checked out the smoke rising from the vehicle. The noxious odor of gas grew fierce, while the fuel tank leaked, spilling the dangerous liquid onto the ground around them.

"This can't be good." Luther stomped against the remaining glass of the window, cleared the hole and tried to unlatch the belt. Unable to reach it, his panic took hold.

"Somebody help me," he hollered out as people had gathered on the bridge, stood there, and just watched. "Come and help, he's stuck." Bellowing got not further response from the rubber-neckers.

A spark erupted from the engine crushed into the concrete, and flames started to rise.

"Come on, wake up, I have to get you out of here." The man moved a little and moaned, still not conscious.

"Help me out here, buddy. Undo your belt. I have to get you out. This thing's gonna blow."

The man stopped moving.

"Goddammit." The flames grew and burned ferociously. Luther choked. The cab filled with smoke. The bottom of his foot started to sting like mad. He looked inside and found the flames had reached the man.

The pain shot up Luther's leg as the flame crept over the trapped victim's limb. A surge of energy washed over him, and he tried to lift the car.

"Come on, come on. Help me." His own screams filled the bottom of his throat, his teeth were clenched. He used every ounce of brute force he could muster and pushed the weight of the vehicle with his hands. He braced himself on sturdy legs and felt the car start to lift. His strength excelled. With one final jolt, he shoved the car over, and it landed on the tires. The fire blazed.

"Christ, that fuckin' hurts." White-hot pain shot through his legs. He grabbed the tight belt, yanked hard, and ripped the latch open, pulling the man out of the vehicle. He dragged him away from the wreck to safety, but the pants of the victim went up in flames. Luther set the injured man on the ground, dropped to his knees, slapped the fire along his legs, and extinguished his pants. From the corner of his eye, he registered flashes.

The man groaned, but remained listless.

"Can somebody get down here? He's hurt." Sirens blared. Luther looked up to the bridge. An ambulance pulled to a stop. In minutes, the paramedics climbed down the hill with a gurney and tended to the victim.

"Christ, that burns." Luther's eyes watered as blistering heat set fire to every nerve in his body. He staggered back. The farther he stumbled away, the more the pain eased. Desperate to avoid any more of the empathic pain, he turned to leave, wanting to put as much distance between the victim and himself as possible.

"Hey, mister, are you hurt, too?" A third paramedic scuttled down the hill and approached him with a kit.

"I-I don't think so." He patted his legs to show he hadn't burned. Still coughing, he eased himself onto the ground and sat.

"Were you in the car, too?"

"No, I was down here, on a walk when I saw him crash."

"You saved his life?"

"I guess so." He shrugged in disbelief.

"That was amazing. Looks like you're a real live hero, sir." The medic pulled out an oxygen mask and placed it over Luther's mouth.

"I wouldn't say that." He glanced up to the smoke-filled sky.

***

THE WALK back to the hotel seemed to take forever. The pay it forward rule was absolute, this much he remembered. Luther snuck away from the accident scene before the police could interview him. He returned to his room and took a shower.

The facecloth, slathered with lemon verbena in the hot shower, proved no match against the grime and gasoline of the fire. Eager to wash it all away, he scrubbed his skin until it stung, a labor-intensive feat. Grateful for the nailbrush in the complimentary bathroom kit, he scoured the black beneath his fingernails. Under the vigorous spray of the jets, he processed the fiery event, stunned at his own reaction. Luther had never been in a situation of life and death before, that is, until his own untimely demise.

"Gabrielle, where the hell are you?" Towel drying his hair, he sat in the chair, still pissed off.

"I'm here." She materialized and stood in the doorway.

"Care to tell me why you disappeared?"

"You had to do that on your own. I couldn't be there to lead you."

"Convenient."

"You did good, Luther, and saved a man's life."

"It's not like I had a choice. No one else would help."

"It was more than most humans would have. You were remarkable." Gabrielle walked to the bed and pulled the covers down.

"What are you up to?" Suspicious, he didn't move.

"It's time to rest, Luther. Day two took a lot out of your body."

"Do you plan to join me?" With caution, he eased his way onto the bed, avoiding any physical contact.

"Entrapment is not an angel's way, Luther. Trust me, you're safe. Get some rest. You earned it."

***

A LOUD buzz roused him from a sound sleep. His body heavy and hard to move. The sound beside his head grew louder. Luther opened his eyes and saw the iPhone vibrating on the nightstand.

"I thought I lost that stupid thing." A flashback of yesterday, he remembered he had tossed it aside at the accident scene and didn't go back to look for it afterward.

"You need to read your message, Luther." Gabrielle sat in the chair, with knitted brows and pursed lips.

"I finished the empathy part?" Hopeful, he grabbed the noisy thing and blinked hard to focus on it.

STRIKE ONE.

"What the fu—?"

"You'd better look at this." She tossed a newspaper onto the bed beside him.

Irritation flooded him, and he stretched his stiff neck side-to-side. He sat up and read the front page. At the sight of the huge, full color picture, his mouth fell open.

The headline read: *Mysterious hero saves man's life and disappears. Who is he?*

The picture, of him when he pulled the man out of the car, had been plastered right there in the daily news for all to see. The angle showed his face, or rather, the face of the human body he was in.

"I got a strike for saving someone's life? I don't get it." Rage consumed him, and he whipped the paper across the room.

"You didn't get the strike for the good deed, but received it because you were recognized for it. This is not anonymous, this...is fame."

"This is bullshit. I didn't pose for that. I didn't talk to anyone or even know they took the picture."

"Nonetheless, Luther, it is a strike. Metatron has ruled it so. I am sorry."

"Yeah, well he's already made it clear he's no fan of mine, so what's the point in a good deed if it's gonna get me put away?" He rubbed his temples and tried to pull back his anger.

"I realize how discouraged you must feel, but time is ticking. It is day three, and you haven't completed the empathy task yet."

"I can't do this. It's too hard." He dropped back onto his pillow like a rock.

"You can and you will. Get up." Although her tone sounded curt, the prompting of her hands when she pulled him to his feet was gentle and encouraging.

He gave a heavy sigh and gazed into the brilliant blue of her eyes, mesmerized by the peace they held. "Tell me what to do next."

***

"WHEN WE just appear places, it makes me nauseous." He scanned the hallway of the hospital and gripped his stomach in an attempt to sooth it.

"We have limited time. I assumed you would want to utilize every precious moment to ensure your success." Gabrielle stood beside him. Her proximity had become familiar, in a dangerous way.

"Good point. Where am I supposed to go now?"

"The room at the end of the hall, on the right."

"And then what?" He turned to face her, but she'd disappeared. "That gets on my nerves. Not even so much as a goodbye?"

Just go, Luther. Her voice filled his ears.

"Fine." He hurried down the hall and stopped in the doorway. There were two hospital beds, one empty and the other behind a partially drawn curtain.

"Hello?"

"Yes, I'm awake. Please come in." The shaky voice behind the cloth barrier sounded faint.

Unsure, Luther approached the bed and pulled the curtain back. There lay a man, bandaged up with casts on his arm and both legs. He had a swollen face, covered with black and blue bruises, cuts, and gashes—the blunt image of a man who met with the wrong end of a battering ram.

"It's you?" The man's voice lifted, and he tried to sit up.

"Please, don't get up." Luther moved closer. "How are you?"

"I'm alive, thanks to you. What's your name?" The brown of his eyes were mostly hidden behind his swollen lids.

"My name? It's Luth— um, John, my name is John." Luther looked behind him, leery of the first strike. He didn't want another.

"Well, John, it's a pleasure to meet you. My name is Jason." With the man's right arm held up, suspended in traction, instead, he offered his left hand, and Luther accepted the gesture and shook it.

"I'm glad you're okay. Are you, uh, will you be...?" Careful not to upset him, he looked to his encased legs.

"I'm gonna be fine. The burns are the worst. I have a few fractures but didn't injure my back, thank God."

"That's a relief." He leaned on the end table. His elbow caught the metal bedpan and knocked it over. A loud series of hollow crashes ensued until he stopped it with his foot.

"Oops." With a nervous laugh, he picked it up and held it at a distance with dread, until he realized the pan was clean. Luther placed it back with relief. Tongue-tied and unsure of what else he should say or do, he tucked his hands in his pant pockets, eased his shoulders up to his ears, and then released with a sigh.

"Hey, do you have a minute to stick around?" The animation in the patient's face amazed Luther—the joy he expressed at his presence, despite how beat up he was.

"Yeah, sure, for the moment, I think I'm good." The metal legs of the chair scrapped along the floor as he pulled it up to the side of the bed and sat down.

"I'm so glad you stopped by. I didn't think I'd get the chance to thank you for saving my life."

"You don't have to. I did what anyone else would have done." Humility, a new trait for him, came easier than he thought.

"No one else did. I saw the news reports last night and the paper this morning. There were dozens of people that just stood around and didn't lift a finger. I could have died if it weren't for you and your bravery."

"Bravery." He exhaled noisily. *If this guy had any clue that my real motive was to save my own soul, he wouldn't call me brave.* "Really, it's okay."

A familiar wave of unbearable scalding resurfaced over his legs. That same scorching that made his stomach turn at the accident scene rushed through him. Luther panted from the pain as a veil of sweat broke out on his face and chest. He looked to Jason and found him grimacing and trembling. He gripped his sheets with colorless knuckles.

"Hey, you're in pain." He jumped up, eager to get away from the searing and ran to the nurses' desk down the hall for help.

Twenty minutes later, the nurses left the room, and Gabrielle still hadn't returned, nor did he have an indicator of what he to do next. The blank screen of the phone seemed to taunt him as he stared at it. He glanced down the desolate hallway, past the gurneys lined up along the walls. In spite of his apprehension, he returned to the open door.

"You look like you're doing better today." Cautious, he inched closer to the bed and waited to see if the burning empathy would return. Instead, a pleasant numbness filled his legs.

"Morphine, I hated the thought of it, but nothing else would stop the pain." Sprawled out flat on the bed, his puffy eyes looked heavy. "I don't like drugs. I can't stand the idea of losing control."

"Huh, that I can relate to." Luther gave a quick glimpse up to the ceiling and sneered.

The wounded man gave a slight chuckle. "You could ask me anything, and I'd tell you. This stuff is kicking my ass." The slur of his words showed the Morphine worked in full force.

Small talk had never been his strong point, unless he was working a female client to swindle. The awkward silence provoked his curiosity.

"Have you had any visitors yet?" He scanned the room and noted the lack of cards and flowers.

"No, I'm alone. There's no one on my next of kin to call."

"No one? No wife, kids, friends?"

"Nope." More childlike in his responses, he moved his head side-to-side, exaggerating his reply.

"Really?"

"I just got into town. I've been away for a long time. I came back, hoping to get my life together again."

"How so?" Luther sat down, intrigued.

"Can you keep a secret?" He chortled then placed his finger against his pressed lips. "Ssshhhh."

"Yeah, of course."

"I just got out of Mexican prison. I wanted to get my girl back."

"You were in prison?"

"Yup." He nodded with the same head bobbing.

"For?" Something seemed vaguely familiar about this man. Luther's stomach began to tense.

"Nothing. I didn't do anything at all."

"Okay, so how did you end up in Mexican prison?" He moved closer studying Jason's expression, listening to every word.

"I was set up. Framed. Sidelined."

"By who?" Luther leaned back into his chair and braced for impact.

"A crooked hotshot with an Armani suit ruined my life."

Frozen in his seat, Luther sat wide-eyed with pressed lips and forced himself to ask more. "What happened?"

"I was in love with the most amazing woman I had ever met. There's never gonna be another like her."

"You loved her?" This wasn't news to him, but it fuelled his motive years ago.

"More than life. The day I lost her, I wanted to die. Even breathing hurt, like I couldn't get any air. That slimy snake, the conniving bastard set me up and took my lady."

Jason's eyes grew dark, and his expression became fierce, then his stare grew vacant fixed on the wall at the other side of the room. Luther sat very still and quiet, terrified the man would recognize him.

"Oh, John. I'm sorry, buddy. I shouldn't ramble on about my problems. You didn't come here for that," he slurred and shifted back to his kind smile. Jason looked to him.

"No, it's okay, go on."

"Have you ever been in love?"

Unable to give an honest answer, he nodded his head and encouraged him to continue.

"We were both so in love with each other. This weasel set his eyes on her, he...I didn't realize until—" Jason burst into tears and sobbed like a baby. The heartbreak hit Luther like a Mac truck.

"I had it all planned to propose to her that night. I had the ring; her favorite burnt orange roses, sangria, every imaginable detail. I decided, wouldn't it be romantic...?" Whimpers were followed by him starting to doze a little.

"Romantic to pop the question in Mexico?" Luther prompted him.

"Yeah, Mexico. We went for a week, had this great little cabana on the beach. I had it all set up, candles, dinner, this fantastic Mariachi band. It was perfect." Jason stared up at the ceiling with a gleam in his eye while he babbled.

"So, uh, what happened?" Luther didn't need to ask, he knew.

"The hotel sent a cabana boy with an urgent message that she needed to come to the hotel right away for a phone call. Within five minutes after she left, thank God she did, the Federales showed up, ten of them, with rifles, dogs, you name it."

"Go on." This part, Luther had in reality never heard about. No one had.

Jason turned to him with such hurt in his eyes. "They beat me within an inch of my life. I remember lying face down on the beach, blood and sand filled my mouth, not one part of me didn't hurt." He shook his head, unable to finish. "Anyway, they said they found a ton of American money, pot, cocaine, and guns stashed all over the cabana. I got nailed for it, and they threw me in jail. They wouldn't let me call anyone."

A shimmer of chills rolled down his spine. "They beat you?"

"That's an understatement." Jason brushed his hair to the side and revealed a deep, long purple scar above his ear.

"You didn't get your phone call?"

"Huh, their legal system is way different than ours. You're guilty, period. I had no allies there, and without money to pay the guards...." The brims of his eyes were red, his voice, strained and gruff. The pain consumed him and, in turn, devoured Luther.

"I was an aspiring artist. Every penny I had, which wasn't much, I sank into that trip and her ring. I got her the most incredible, heart-shaped emerald ring, her birthstone, white gold.... I'm lucky to have gotten out alive. A few times, I didn't think I would make it."

This poor shell of a man poured his heart and soul out under the influence of painkillers. Luther heard the whole story, for the first time. Jason told it in such detail, it felt as though he had been right there, living it with him. The empathic curse broke him right then and there.

"You know the worst part, John?"

Luther waited, he couldn't take much more.

"I never got to say goodbye to her. The ring disappeared. They probably stole it. To this day, I don't know what she thought. That maybe I left her there? I don't know. I may never know. Did that jerk even love her? He didn't strike me as a kind or devoted man."

"I'm so sorry, Jason, I had no idea." With his head into his hands, it felt as though some cord inside his chest had snapped in two. Guilt permeated his mind. His soul ached.

"Don't apologize, you saved my life. You just met me. That selfish piece of crap on the other hand...." Jason smiled again. "Wow, you see, this is why I don't like drugs. I sound like a long-winded idiot." His head dropped to the side, and his eyes shut.

"Hey, Jason." Luther shook him gently to rouse him. "I have one more question, okay?"

"Sure, ask away." He laughed with heavy eyes.

"How did you get out of there?"

"That's the wild part. After five of the longest years of my life, I was sure I would be there until I died. Two days ago, they came in and got me, cleaned me up, transported me to the American Embassy, and the next thing you know, I'm on a plane back here."

"Why two days ago?"

"They weren't real talkative, ya know? They spoke in Spanish at the embassy. I could only make out parts of it, but it sounded like a man here paid my way."

"A man? Someone you know?"

"I don't know anyone with that kind of money. It would have taken a bundle to get me out of there. In Mexico, money is the only way to buy a guy freedom." Out for the count, he started to snore, his last words fading when he drifted off.

Chapter Ten

"DAD PAID to get Jason out, didn't he?" Luther stood in the middle of the hospital parking lot and called out for Gabrielle.

"Yes." She appeared. "He did."

"He said he knew what I'd done." Shaking his head in disbelief, he sat down on a barrier.

"I may have arranged to have the money put there, but I didn't include any drugs or weapons. I swear to God, I didn't do that. I didn't want them to kill him, only to get him out of the way long enough to…." Weighted down by his guilty conscience, he hung his head as though it weighed a hundred pounds.

"Long enough to steal the woman he loved. All because you spotted another conquest for yourself."

"Yeah, I guess you're right."

"So, Luther, the question is, if you didn't put the rest of the stuff there, who did?"

The ability to recall the details of that fateful night was rusty, until his panic set in.

"I booked a flight to go down for business and meet some clients. I made it a little vacation."

"Alone?" Gabrielle's tone remained flat.

"No. Marvin came down with me."

"I see."

"He came up with the idea to stash the money to frame him and call the police."

"Then what?"

"Marvin knew some guys. I withdrew the money from the bank, and he took care of it." The proverbial light turned on. "We sat in the hotel bar while we waited. Jasmine went to the desk, I *bumped into her*, and the rest is history."

"It would seem so." Disapproval saturated her voice and her stare.

"I had no idea. I thought, he'd get picked up, lose his passport, maybe be detained until he made a call."

"The ramifications of our actions are not always clear to us right away."

"You can say that again. I can't even imagine, for you to go through—losing Jasmine that way." Silence devoured him, and his head throbbed. Confusion. Sorrow.

"Luther, you should check your phone now." Gabrielle gave a soft smile.

The vibration in his pocket barely registered until she pointed it out. He pulled it out with weakened fingers. A whimper rushed through his lungs as he read the screen.

Second task is completed. The relief he expected to feel had gone amiss. In its place, a dark cloud of shame enveloped him.

"Gabrielle, I have to find some way to make this right."

"I know, Luther. You haven't read your next task."

He glanced back at the screen, it read: *Task three: you must demonstrate compassion.*

"This, I'll figure out later." He stood up. A renewed sense of purpose energized his stiff body.

"You have somewhere you intend to go?"

"Yes, I'm gonna see Jasmine."

"Luther, that isn't a good idea. If you reveal who you are to her, Metatron will revoke your chance at redemption."

"Believe me, I realize that. It's a good thing I have experience in how to work around the truth and pose as someone other than me. It became an acquired skill of mine."

Gabrielle turned and faced him with a one-sided grin. She held her hand out, and he took it.

***

"WHO IS IT?" The voice box on the iron gate sounded out.

"Flower delivery for Ms. Jasmine Trudel."

"Uh, fine, come up to the house." The electronic lock clicked, and the gate creaked open.

While he waited for her to answer the door, he looked over his shoulder to make sure his angelic sidekick remained invisible.

The clack of the lock as it turned seemed strange to hear from the outside. Behind the heavy wooden door that swung open stood a pale, gaunt version of the woman he expected to see.

"Who are they from?" The puffiness around her eyes and upper lip gave her away. He had interrupted a long overdue emotional letdown.

"There's a card." Holding it up, he gave a smile. Part of him hoped she could see through his disguise. So much of him wanted to take her into his arms and hold her tight, tell her the entirety of his hellish nightmare, no matter how much he brought it on himself.

Taped to the box with a red ribbon was the mini envelope. Her face lacked enthusiasm or movement, but she opened it and read the card aloud.

From an old friend, who can't wait to see you. "Is there a name or an address? How am I supposed to know who this is?" A slight quiver of her bottom lip caused him to second guess his plan.

"There is a...second delivery scheduled for tomorrow." Quick thinking, but maybe not well thought out. He grasped at straws.

"Is that so? I won't be here tomorrow. I have to move out." Letting out a heavy sigh, she looked down; Luther rubbed his chest to ease the discomfort of the discouragement that consumed her heart.

"If you want to give me your new address, I'll make sure you get it. I'll deliver it myself." Eager to get his foot in the door, he feared he didn't come across as smooth as he planned.

"You're very sweet. Hang on, I'll get you a tip. Please wait here." She left the door wide open and disappeared down the hall. Luther stepped inside and canvassed his home with disgust.

My body isn't even cold, and he kicked her out. How did I let that heartless son-of-a-bitch do this to me? To her? Dammit. The walls were bare, pictures stacked on the floor, and boxes taped and piled all around.

Eager to explore it all in the brief time he had, Luther walked into the den and took in the unsightly scene. Almost every personal item had been packed, except one silver framed picture above the fireplace mantel, a photograph of him and Jasmine, in Mexico, the week he stole her away and ruined Jason's life.

The arrogance in your expression indeed did not denote love. Gabrielle remained unseen but managed to shoot a dagger to his heart.

Unable to respond to the brutal but oh so true observation, he trailed his fingers over the image, regret saturated his soul.

"Oh, there you are." Jasmine startled him, and he swung around to face her. "I know this isn't much, but it's all I have on me." She held out a five-dollar bill and gave him a gentle smile.

"No, no, thank you. I couldn't take that."

"Please." She waved it with insistence.

"Alright, thank you." To accept it from her allowed him the chance to touch her hand. The softness of her skin sent a ripple of warmth through his chest.

Awkward silence filled the room, and Jasmine fidgeted, then headed for the front door. "I appreciate the delivery. I have a lot to finish up here."

"Have you done all this packing alone?"

"Yes, it's just me."

Back at the front entrance where she stood, he held the door open, not ready to leave.

"You shouldn't have to do all this by yourself, not in your condition." In an attempt to find the baby bump, he glimpsed at her baggy shirt.

"My condition?" Wide-eyed, she spoke with a cracked voice. "How would you know what my condition is?" Jasmine clutched her stomach and stared him down with narrowed eyes.

"I don't...what I meant to say, uh...you look so pale." Fumbling through words, he needed a fast recovery. "I figured you must have the flu or something." Out came the batting of his eyes in hopes to sidetrack the conversation.

"Pale? I am? Yes, I suppose I'm not at my best this week."

"Maybe, can I offer you some help? To pack, I mean?"

"Help? You don't even know me." The sudden onset of her waxen complexion was followed by Jasmine gripping the door. She appeared off balance.

"Hey, are you okay?" The words hadn't quite left his mouth as she collapsed. Catching her, he scooped her up and brought her over to the couch. "Jasmine? Hey, honey, wake up. Jasmine?" The color of her lips had faded, and he couldn't wake her at all.

Chapter Eleven

"DO YOU feel better?" Her eyes fluttered open, which brought Luther some relief. The cool damp cloth he patted her face down with had grown warm.

"You're the delivery guy?" Jasmine tried to sit up and appeared so frail.

"It's okay, take it easy." Luther handed her a glass of water and adjusted the throw cushion behind her back.

"Thank you. I don't know what happened." She put the glass to her lips with a trembling hand.

"You fainted. When did you last eat?"

With a vacant stare, she glanced at her wristwatch. "I guess it's been awhile."

"Let me fix you a snack."

"I've been too much trouble already, it's alright."

"Jazzy, I don't mind. You need food." When she grabbed his wrist, he stood up.

"What did you call me?" The quivering of her bottom lip made him stutter.

"J-Jasmine? That is your name, isn't it?"

"I could have sworn you said…. Never mind, my head's a little messed up."

"I'll be right back." A fast escape to the kitchen.

You almost blew it hotshot.

I know.

In a frenzy, he gathered her favorite snack foods, put the kettle on, and got the silver tray ready.

Luther, this is a big mistake.

It's all right. She needs to eat, have you seen her? She looks so sick.

It's almost time to go. Make it quick.

Luther rushed down the hall, careful not to spill anything. "Here we go."

Jasmine had pulled a sweater over her shoulders and trembled.

"You're cold?" Over on the recliner, he spotted his favorite chemise throw. In a flash, he draped it over her and placed the tray in her lap. "Your feast, Mademoiselle."

"Tea? You made me tea as well?"

"Yes, with honey." Pleased with his care giving skills, he sat at her side.

"It's odd." The confusion in her eyes followed her subtle interrogation. "You seem to know your way around this house. You've managed to pick all my favorite snacks and tea with honey." Raised brows, she shook her head. "Do we know each other? Have we met? You seem so familiar to me."

"No, we don't. I, uh...I get that a lot."

"What's your name?"

"J-John."

"It's nice to meet you John. You're like a guardian angel." With a slight giggle, she picked up the teacup and took a sip.

"It's perfect."

"Ah," he sighed with relief. "I see some color back in your face. Should I call a doctor or someone?"

"Oh, I'm fine. I just over did it, and you were right, I neglected to eat. That won't happen again." She devoured the sliced fruit first then went on to the ham sandwich, ending with the cheese and crackers. It amazed him how fast she gobbled it all up. Most times, Jasmine tended to be a dainty eater.

Luther, it's time.

Just, wait a minute.

Now.

Okay.

"I'm sorry, I have to go. Will you be okay?"

"I'm much better, thank you."

"Good, I'm glad."

"I wish I had some way I could repay your kindness."

"There is one way." The corners of his mouth pulled back, her guard was down.

"There is?"

"I have a few friends, they...owe me a favor. I would consider it even if you let them come, help you pack, and move to your new place."

"I couldn't, it's too much." She set the cup down and shook her head, her cheeks growing red.

"Well then, I suppose I'll have to come back and do it myself."

"John, I can't let you do that."

"I'd feel much better about leaving if I knew you were looked after. Please let me help."

"Wow, I don't know what to say."

"Yes, is all I need to hear."

"Fine, then. I'd be happy to have some extra hands." The most gracious smile lit up her ice blue eyes. Jasmine tucked her chin down, the same way she used to when they first dated, shy.

"I'll have them here in a few hours. Promise me you won't go and overdo it again?"

Jasmine let out a big sigh. "I promise." She rubbed her stomach.

"That second delivery, I'll bring it to your new address tomorrow. Until then, my friends will take care of everything for you." He grabbed the pen and paper from on top of a box beside the couch and handed it to her for the information.

"Your kindness is great, and your timing couldn't be better, thank you."

Luther collected her hand and gave a gentle kiss on the back of her fingers. The desire to be more forward got interrupted with the shrill sound of Gabrielle's voice in his head.

Luther.

***

"THAT'S A cute stunt." Gabrielle's legs moved so swift, he had to jog to keep up with her.

"I couldn't leave her like that. She's pregnant."

"My job is to guide you, but I'm not here to run interference when Metatron is ready to clamp down on your antics."

"What's his problem?"

Gabrielle stopped short and glared at him with cynical eyes. "This week is not to get you hooked up with your old girlfriend, Luther."

"I never thought it was."

"If I hadn't been there, would you have gone on to seduce her?"

"What? Where did that come from?"

The cerulean hue of her eyes glowed with fury.

"Hold on a minute." He shook his head and snickered. "Are you jealous?"

"Don't be ridiculous. I'm an archangel on a mission. Why would your romantic pursuits be of any consequence to me?" Gabrielle swung around and stormed off.

"The tension between us. It's somethin', isn't it?" He chuckled to himself and ran to catch up to her. "I need a favor."

"You need—?" She huffed with annoyance and stopped. "What is it?"

"Can you get me some money?"

"For what?"

"I need to hire movers for Jazz."

Gabrielle let out a heavy sigh and composed herself. "Consider it already done."

"Awesome. Thanks, angel." He offered her a wink and a grin, but they didn't have the effect on her he hoped for. The cold exterior remained.

"The next stop is where, boss?"

"It would appear you have an agenda of your own. Where do you plan to go?"

"To see an old acquaintance. It's time to make this right."

"Acquaintance. Another girlfriend?"

"No, it's not like that. How fast can you get me to Montana?"

Chapter Twelve

"THIS ISN'T Giselle's house. Where are we?" Luther scouted the length of the barren hallway. It didn't look like the same hospital they were in before.

"It's the West Haven Sanatorium."

"I wanted to go to Giselle's house."

"If you haven't learned by now how this works, Luther...." With her hands on her hips, she shot him an annoyed expression.

"Alright. I'm going." He glanced down and discovered himself suited in an orderly's uniform. The trolley in front of him held dozens of paper cups filled with pills. "Which room?"

"Two doors down on the left."

The hall sat empty. His footsteps and the roll of the wheels echoed along the deserted corridor. At the second door on the left, he tried the locked handle then looked through the small glass window. There sat a woman facing the barred window with her back to him. He patted himself down and located keys attached to his belt. After several tries, he found the right key and unlocked the door.

"Excuse me?" He called louder than a whisper so not to startle her. When she didn't respond, he entered the room with the cart.

"I don't want any damned medicine." The curt voice sounded familiar.

Luther approached the woman from behind as he took note of her disheveled, graying hair and the straight jacket wrapped around her. It encased her arms and body.

"Oh, my God, Giselle, is that you?" Astonished, he moved to the window and inspected her.

"Go away." Angry tears streamed down her ashen face.

Gabrielle, what happened here?

Ask her yourself. She is lucid.

"Giselle, it's me, Luth— John, my name is John. I'm a friend."

"I don't have any friends. If I did, he wouldn't have been able to do this to me." She struggled hard, wiggling and pulling at the restrictive garment.

"Who?"

"My son, that ungrateful demon of a child."

"Marvin did this to you?"

"Don't play me. I'm not delusional. Just because you people don't believe me—" She growled through gritted teeth then struggled some more.

"I'm not playing you. I'm...a friend of Luther's." He knelt down to face her, and she snapped her head up with broadened eyes and her mouth ajar. "Luther?"

"Yes, I wanted to make sure you were okay, so I came to speak with you." He cupped her cheek and brushed away a stream of tears.

"You know I'm not crazy?"

"I know. I believe you, Giselle. How did you get here?"

"That evil spawn forged all the papers. He posed as a psychiatrist and had me admitted by ambulance."

"When?"

"Last week when I went to visit him and Beth."

"That's why you left in such a rush?"

"He would never have gotten near me if I hadn't been stupid enough to drink the orange juice he *hand squeezed for his dearest mother,*" she snarled.

"Juice?" Luther rubbed the shaking shoulders of the distraught woman.

"I should have known better. He's never done a damn thing for me ever. Never a simple kindness like make me a drink. It's not his style."

"Why would he do this to you?" Luther blinked hard through the blurry vision of wetness.

"Because I wouldn't stand for his dishonesty, his thievery. He locked me up here to keep me quiet. I told him what he was doing was wrong, and I'd warn them, all of them."

"Who?"

"Jasmine, Jasper, Luther. I found out what he had been up to when I visited him last week."

"But I— Luther died three days ago."

"Lucky for him he didn't live to see my son's treachery."

"What do you mean?"

"Marvin had this set up for months. He forged documents and posed as a lawyer. Poor Beth has no clue. She's next, you know. He'll take every last penny of hers and kick her out of her own home, too. He had brochures for the Caribbean. That deceitful cheat even laughed at me and said he would be on the beach with a tan before any of them knew what hit them. He said I would never be able to warn them because he would leave me here to rot."

"This is unreal." Luther dropped his head into his hands.

"I can't believe this is the son I raised. The unspeakable things he had them do to me here. They treat me like an animal." Giselle struggled in the restraints and burst into tears. She sobbed and gasped for breath. Luther held her tight, his heart breaking along with hers.

To see her like this was unbearable. He reached behind her, unlatched the jacket, and let her arms down.

"Giselle, what did you see him doing a week ago?"

Unable to speak at first, she whimpered.

"It's okay, I won't let anyone hurt you again. I promise." He cupped her cold cheek.

Giselle drew in a long breath then blurted out the rest, "I'm sure if Luther hadn't died, he would have killed him. He planned to take all his money, the houses, the cars, whatever he could get his greedy little hands on. That devil is ruthless."

"Kill him? Marvin planned to kill Luther? Please, Giselle. I need you to slow down and focus for me. What did you see?"

She smoothed her wiry hair back and sucked in a long breath before she spoke. "When I visited a week ago, I stopped by his office to take him out for lunch and found him at the hidden safe in his wall. He had mounds of money, jewelry, and legal papers. I stood in the doorway and watched him. I couldn't believe my eyes."

"You saw him in the safe?"

"The one behind the big painting in his private office. I saw everything. He had a small brown bottle. I don't know what it held, but he hid it in the safe along with the papers, some cigars, and jewelry. I can't remember anything else." She forced her words through clenched teeth and massaged her arms. Luther could feel the ache in her pulled muscles.

"Come on." He stood and pulled her to her feet.

"Where are you taking me? Please, not the electric shock room. It's barbaric. Not again, please," she begged and tugged at his arm.

"Giselle, I'm a friend. I'm not gonna let anyone else hurt you, I promise."

The long walk down the corridor seemed to take forever as he pushed the cart and passed the nurses' station. He held up his ID badge. With a nod, the woman on duty unlocked the electronic door, and he rolled the trolley through.

Uneasy, he pressed the elevator button.

Once he reached the underground garage, he held his hand out and helped Giselle from the inside of the cart. Gabrielle pulled up in a car and opened the door.

"Let's get out of here before anyone sees us." Luther helped Giselle climb into the back seat.

***

THE VIBRATION in his pocket startled him awake. He bolted upright in the hotel bed and swung his head side to side to find the noisy origin.

"It's your phone, genius."

"Yeah, got it." Luther fished through his pants for it. Unsure what to expect, he held the phone and waited.

"Aren't you gonna read it?"

"I thought maybe I'd just wait for lightning to strike me down." He glanced up to the ceiling and drew in a long, deep lungful of air , exhaled and then tapped screen as he held his breath.

Task three is completed.

"You seem surprised." Gabrielle sat on the chair and faced him with one leg crossed over the other.

"I expected breaking someone out of a sanatorium would get me a strike for sure."

"You did it for the right reason, Luther. Giselle didn't belong in there. You showed compassion." A little grin lit up her luminescent eyes.

"Are you proud of me or somethin'?"

"Don't get overconfident, Luther. It was a good deed. You still have more work to do."

"So much for a smile out of you. Day four, right? More than half way there." Energized today, he jumped out of bed, eager to get a move on.

Gabrielle sat silent in the chair her eyes fixed on the floor and avoided his gaze.

"What is it?"

"I need to take you somewhere for more information."

"Okay, so what's with the sad eyes?"

"You won't like it."

"How is that different than anything else these past few days?" He chuckled.

"My judgment would be to wait and not show you until after."

"After what?"

"You complete your tasks and achieve your redemption."

"Gabrielle, I thought we had gotten past all the cryptic talk. What's up?" Luther sat back down on the bed, and the ominous sense of doom returned.

"My concern is if I show you before you finish, it might interfere with...."

With furrowed brows, he gawped and waited to hear the rest. *An archangel giving confession? What an odd moment.* "What?"

"Your focus."

"I don't get it."

In the blink of an eye, Luther looked around to find they were back at the Great Hall.

"Did I do something wrong? I don't have three strikes. Why are we here?"

At the table sat Jeremiel with puckered brows and Metatron with pursed lips.

"You have made good progress so far."

Metatron gave me a compliment?

"So then, why are we here? I only have three days left and still have more to do, don't I?"

In search of his mother, he glanced around in hopes she would be there to greet him. Instead, he found Gabrielle, back in her formal angel attire with wings and all.

"Gabrielle, you have done well in your task to guide your charge. I sense your hesitation in the implementation of your next order."

"Yes Metatron. I am...apprehensive."

"Explain."

"Yes, by all means, explain." Luther glowered as he studied her. "What is this about?"

"This new information, I fear, will lead him astray. His spirit is strong with human ways. My worry is he can be swayed to a dark response."

"You cannot protect him from that. It is his responsibility to adhere to the rules and demonstrate rehabilitation."

"Understood." To see her bow was a first. Not one observation about this angel had suggested subservience to him before.

"For this part of your journey, you will accompany Gabrielle in ethereal body. Your job is to see and hear, and that is all." The sternness of his voice suggested he hadn't earned a place in the good book yet.

"If this is up to me to do, to prove, why does everyone act like I'm a drug addict in the middle of crack central?"

"Your analogy isn't too far from the truth, Luther. Albeit, determination is strong, other negative emotions remain unreserved within you and have the potential to turn you back to your former ways." Jeremiel folded his hands and placed them on the ledger.

"Maybe I'll surprise you all. Time is ticking away. Can we please get on with this?" Impatience flooded him.

"Gabrielle...in spirit. He is not to have access to the physical realm until we see fit to allow the rest of his tasks to be completed."

Up until this point, Luther had started to feel good about himself, but all the talk of doubt made him nervous, as though he housed a demon deep inside that everyone else knew about but him.

***

"WE'RE at the hospital again?"

"It's an obstetrics clinic." Gabrielle moved along the corridor with him at her side.

"Obstet—" A wave of panic rushed over him. "The baby? Is Jasmine okay?"

"She is fine. In fact, I thought you should see this part first to help keep your focus."

"You sound like a mother hen."

"Here." She motioned to the closed examination room. "Go through that door."

Luther put his hand out to push open the door, but it went through like it didn't exist.

"What the—?"

"You have no body. Go through, it's fine."

"Sure it is." Luther eyed the impossible blockade, collected his nerve, and jumped through the door. "That's not so bad."

He looked back and laughed. Gabrielle followed him in, graceful as usual.

With mixed emotions, he glanced around the room, overpowered when he saw the solemn Jasmine on the hospital bed, her feet in the stirrups. "Oh, I don't need to see this, do I?"

"You won't witness the internal examine." His angel pointed to the monitor at Jasmine's side and evaporated.

"There you go again. Not much for hello and goodbye, are you?" he called out to the ceiling.

"How is our new mommy today?" A middle-aged man entered the room in blue medical scrubs and a paper mask hanging from his neck.

"A little tired but much better." Jasmine caressed her baby bump.

"Let's see how our little patient is, shall we?"

A proverbial lump formed in Luther's non-existent throat. He moved to Jasmine's side and waited for the monitor to light up.

The doctor lifted her gown, exposed her swollen belly, and slathered clear gel all over it.

How far along is she? I never noticed her belly.
How much attention did you pay to her, Luther?
Fine. Point taken.

With the handheld probe, he rubbed in circular motions. The speakers crackled with the sounds of the device grazing along her skin.

On one spot of her tummy, the doctor paused and fiddled with the volume control on the base with his free hand and turned it louder.

"There you go, Mom. There's your little miracle." The pearl-like strand curved in the black moving picture, and the exquisite thump of the fast heartbeat sounded out.

"My baby?" Jasmine's eyes welled up, and she bit her lower lip.

Luther knew this face. Her, *I'm happy but-can't-let-myself-smile,* face. Her hands trembled over her belly as her lips quivered.

"Is he okay?" Her voice shook.

"It's too soon to know the sex, but your baby's heartbeat is just right. The little white dots along there, that's the spine, formed to perfection. The baby looks great, Jasmine."

"Thank God." She nestled her head back against the seat, relief filling her face.

"With the noted date of your last menses and this scan, I would say you're close to seven weeks."

Silent as she lay on the gurney, she nodded and cradled her stomach.

"Would you like me to print out a picture? You could show the baby's father."

Shock filled Jasmine's face. Luther stood at her side and waited for the wave to hit.

Jasmine clamped her hand over her mouth and muffled a whimper as a tear spilled down her cheek.

"Jasmine, are you all right?" It was evident the poor guy had no clue about her situation.

"I'm fine, yes. I would love some pictures, thank you." The ceiling tiles maintained her attention until the doctor made a fast exit from the room. The weight of the doctor's head seemed to force his chin down to his chest.

After he left, Jasmine held the picture in her hand and just stared at it. Her eyes held the same empty expression she wore at his graveside. The helplessness that consumed Luther made it impossible not to react.

"Jasmine, I'm here babe. I'm so sorry you have to do this alone."

The painful urge to caress her face overwhelmed him as he watched. "Please hear me."

A familiar winged apparition appeared on the other side of Jasmine. Azrael put his hand on her shoulder as she stayed still and pallid.

"What the hell do you want? You can't take her. No, I won't let you." Luther lunged at him.

"I am here to counsel, Luther. It is not Jasmine's time." Azrael held up his hand and stopped Luther on the spot in mid air. Luther couldn't touch him, as though an invisible field held him back.

"You're not gonna kill her?"

"I do not kill humans, Luther. I counsel them in grief and transport when they cross over. Jasmine is in bereavement and requires my presence, which is all, I assure you."

You have an ethereal body. You are on a different plane of existence. She cannot see, hear, or feel you anymore, only the memories she is left with. Let Azrael do his job. She is safe. I promise. Gabrielle's hushed voice stayed with him as he watched the mother of his child.

Jasmine lay there for the longest time. She took in a deep breath, got up, tossed the hospital gown on the gurney, and got dressed.

"Gabrielle, I wish I could hold her and tell her it's gonna be alright."

"I am not able to grant that wish, Luther."

"Even as John? She won't know it's me, please?"

"I am not authorized to do so. You still have work to do. I'm sorry."

"I never realized how much she loved me."

"You never stuck around long enough to figure it out."

Azrael vanished.

The sadness in her eyes returned. Jasmine let go of her baby bump, gripped the edge of the gurney, and steadied herself as she broke down. She heaved and sobbed for several minutes, unable to gain control of herself.

Luther turned to his distraught Jasmine once more and fell to his knees beside her, weeping for the first time he could remember since his mother's death.

"I don't deserve your tears. I'm a selfish shit and never gave you half of what you needed. I'm a coward and was afraid to open up, missing out on the best thing in my life. I am so sorry, Jasmine. I did love you, I swear. I still do."

Luther reached for her hand and gasped as she stepped right through him and rushed out the door.

Chapter Thirteen

"WHERE ARE we?" Unable to muster any emotion, Luther lowered his shoulders and his voice fell flat.

"Where you need to be, but please, Luther, remember Jasmine and your baby. This part will be most difficult for you to hear."

"You're still worried I'll lose it. It's okay. I promise. I'll keep it together. I don't want to blow it." Luther took her hand and held it with a gentle squeeze. Gabrielle stared down where their fingers were intertwined, confusion filling her eyes.

"It's time." She pulled out of his grasp and crossed her arms, looking at him with stern eyes. She glanced forward and prompted him to look ahead.

A number of people sat in the row of metal chairs lined along the wall across from a large, glassed-in desk. He glanced around and took every detail in. A disheveled woman with a peek-a-boo crop top and a too short skirt slumped in her seat. She chewed gum with her mouth wide open and primped her wild, platinum curls. Beside her sat an older woman who clutched her purse and cried. Farther down, a teen in a denim jacket held his head in his hands, and a dirty, middle-aged, scruffy man sat with his arms folded. The man had dosed off and snored like mad.

"Is this the police station?"

"Yes. Follow me. We must go downstairs to the basement floor."

Luther did as she told him, and they walked down the dingy staircase and exited the door.

"No more elevators? That's a shame, although this stairwell is just as nasty." Another vacant hallway with several doors along the corridor. "What are we doing here?"

"Going to the Forensics lab."

The third door on the right, Gabrielle nodded for Luther to enter first, and then she followed.

"What does this have to do with—?"

"Just listen." The vibrant blue of her eyes had muted somewhat. Her brows were knitted, and she pointed to the two men in white lab coats who examined a file and debated the contents.

"The coroner ruled this death asphyxiation. The poor bugger choked to death. Why did you drudge all this up?" the pudgier forty-something man with salt and pepper hair bantered.

"I need you to keep an open mind, Jared."

"Okay, I'm all ears."

"The first detective on scene observed the facial edema but also noticed his nail beds. Look at these post mortem photographs." He flung the open file on the metal table in front of them. "He may have died from asphyxiation, but the facial edema suggested an acute dose, and the blood work will certainly confirm as the nail beds suggest, a chronic exposure to poison." The younger fair-haired man spoke low and fast.

"What is this about?" Luther turned to Gabrielle.

She gave a stern look and shushed him.

"Someone was poisoning the poor bastard little by little." The older man nodded in agreement as they studied the photos on the table.

"How he ingested the poison is difficult to determine, but the assailant would have had access to items he used on a regular basis."

"If we find the motive, it will be easier to track down the source."

"Does this mean we investigate this death as a homicide?" The blonde man re-examined the file on the tabletop.

"Yes. If the evidence we're looking at is correct, he didn't choke to death. He received a fatal dose of poison. It's possible his killer escalated this for a reason."

"The evidence collected at the hotel room turned out to be minimal at best."

"That would be because they ruled the death asphyxiation. Someone tampered with the evidence. All the pieces of the puzzle aren't here." The older man, Jared, grimaced.

"I think you're right. See here, this part of the coroner's report doesn't match up with the scene of his death." He pointed to the paper, and his partner hunched over and read it.

"The coroner found champagne in his system, ingested right before time of death, but the report doesn't state they found any at the scene."

"Okay, no bottle. But there were small shards of black glass found on the dinner plate, table, and carpet. However, there's no indication of what got broken or where it disappeared to." The young lad had a badge on his belt.

Luther leaned in and read the name. *Smith,* straightened his back and scrubbed his face with his hands. "What color glass is a bottle of champagne?"

Jared tapped his chin with his index finger and glanced up in thought. "It depends on the brand. Some do come in black bottles."

"I will do a search for brands, compare the glass composition to manufacturers. We will find a match."

"Good. I think you're onto something. This all still sounds fishy to me. We will need to get search warrants for home and business. The hotel room has already been cleaned and used since. I doubt we will find much, but we can get the warrant for the hotel again."

Jared flipped through a few more pages and glanced at Smith. "The paper trail is sufficient enough. Did you get a court order to exhume him?"

"Already in the process. The judge should have it signed by this afternoon."

"So, it's official; accidental death is ruled out. We have a potential homicide." Jared huffed.

"Once we get the toxicology reports back, that will be determined. In the meantime, we need to get over to the morgue as soon as the body arrives. The coroner needs to re-do the autopsy."

"How did you get wind of this, anyway?" The stout man scraped his fingers across his five o'clock shadow.

"The emergency room doctor filed a report, suspicion of poisoning, after he took blood samples the night before he died."

"What do you expect to see in the toxicology?"

"I'm not an expert on it, but the hospital report indicated the doctor had searched for verification of poisoning. The victim had Mee's lines in his nails. The physician on call requested a test for arsenic."

***

"SO, I SEE why you were so worried about my reaction." Luther sat down on the park bench.

"Yes, the details of your death change your mission for redemption."

Luther snapped his head up with annoyance. "Why? I still have to earn it, don't I?"

"Yes, however, this is a distraction we hadn't anticipated. It could throw you off course."

"Well, I'm gonna have to stick to the tasks at hand, aren't I?"

Gabrielle nodded with a smile.

"I know, I'm almost out of time."

"What will you do?"

"If I wasn't about to lose my soul for eternity, I would have killed the bastard who murdered me with my bare hands." Void of emotion, it took the last of his will to force one corner of his mouth to retreat with his sarcasm.

"Well then, let me rephrase, since eternal damnation hangs in the balance. How do you intend to respond?"

"I'm not sure yet. I can't let him get away with it."

"Choose with care, Luther." Gabrielle sat beside him and placed her hand over his.

"If I didn't know any better, I might get the impression my angel is crushing on me." He winked.

"To demonstrate compassion for someone does not denote lust, you arrogant—" She pulled her hand back with a sneer.

"Relax. Can't a dead man have a sense of humor?"

"Very funny." She crossed her arms over her chest.

"Hey, what time is it?"

"Two o'clock."

"I need to get to Jasmine's and help her move."

"You hired movers for that."

"Is it your goal to want to waste more time arguing with me?" He stood up, tucked his hands in his pockets. He pursed his lips in dismay.

"Very well."

***

"THANK YOU so much, John, for all your help. You saved my life." Jasmine pointed to the corner, and he carried the box of dishes and placed it with her other belongings.

"You're looking much healthier today."

"I'm feeling better and haven't missed a meal since." She winked and patted his arm. "I promise."

The doorbell chimed.

"Oh, the security gate is left open for the movers. That must be them at the door." Jasmine excused herself and opened the front door.

"Dad?" Luther mouthed and froze on the spot.

"Hello, Jasmine." Jasper smiled and gave her a tender hug.

"What are you doing here?"

"I'm here to bring you home, sweetheart." Jasper's mouth fell open when he glanced around the bare house. He leaned heavy on his cane with a slight wobble.

"I know, it looks so different." Jasmine tucked her hand over his free arm and coaxed him to follow her.

"There is someone I would like you to meet. Dad, this is my very own guardian angel." She led him to Luther. "This gentleman has been a godsend. He sent the movers here to help me out."

"Thank you, son, for all your help." Jasper held his hand out and offered a smile.

Luther stood still, speechless.

"Is something wrong?" Jasper looked to Jasmine when he got no response.

"I don't think so. John?" She reached over and rubbed his arm. "Are you okay?"

"Uh." He shook off the shock. "Yeah, yeah. I'm sorry, you caught me in a little bit of a daze." He accepted Jasper's firm handshake and didn't let go right away. "It's a pleasure to meet you, sir."

Jasper leaned closer and stared into Luther's eyes. "Have we met before?"

"No! Um, I don't believe so." Luther pulled back his hand, ran his fingers through his hair, and looked around the room to avoid his father's piecing stare.

"Forgive me, you seem so familiar."

The doorbell chimed again.

"My goodness, it's hectic in here. Please excuse me, gentleman." She left Luther and his father as they stood face-to-face.

"Can I help you?" Jasmine stood at the open door and was confronted by four uniformed officers and a plain-clothed man who held out a detective badge.

"Miss Jasmine Trudel?"

"Yes, that's me."

"You need to come with us to the police station for a few questions."

"About what?"

"The death of Luther Evans."

"What?" she cried. Luther ran to her side, and Jasper followed in quick pursuit.

"Hold on a minute, have you got a warrant?"

"Yes, to search the premises. Everyone step outside and don't touch anything else in this house." The detective handed her a warrant. Three officers entered the house and began their search.

"There has to be some mistake." Her voice cracked.

"I'm afraid not, Miss Trudel. We need you to come down to the station for questioning."

"Wait, for what? You can't arrest her." Luther pushed him back from Jasmine.

"Stand back, sir, or you will be arrested for interference with a murder investigation."

"What the hell?"

"John." Jasmine turned to him, tears racing down her sallow cheeks. "Please, don't get yourself into trouble over me. I haven't done anything wrong. I will go with them and get this sorted out."

"See here, gentlemen, take your hands off my daughter-in-law." Jasper stood tall and rapped his cane on the floor.

"Jasper, it's okay. It's gonna be fine."

"But...." Helpless, he stood by and watched them escort her out the door and into the back of the squad car.

"Please, she's pregnant. Don't hurt her." Luther's dad pleaded as his chin quivered.

"I'm okay."

"Gabrielle?" He summoned her with a scowl as he headed out the gate.

Chapter Fourteen

"I NEED TO hear what they talk to her about first."

"Fine, but in spirit. No physical contact."

"Trust me, I won't be stupid at a police station, and the one way I can hear, is to be unseen anyway. I'm fine with that."

Gabrielle stood at his side behind the glass observation window as the detective questioned Jasmine.

"I understand from sources that Luther Evans had been quite the ladies' man."

"What's your point?" The cool, fearless exterior she carried in the interview surprised Luther. He didn't observe this often in Jasmine, but she had a real edge to her at the moment. The detective handed her a glass of water.

"My point is, you had plenty of reason to be angry with him. He screwed around on you."

"I love him," she barked and then paused. Her narrowed eyes widened and began to glisten as shock filled her porcelain face. "I mean, I *loved* him." Her voice trembled.

"Love and hate are divided by a fine line."

"Perhaps to you because you're a cynical pessimist. I loved him. There were no two ways about it." Jasmine held the glass with shaky hands.

"Our sources say, he had been with another woman the night he died, right before your engagement party."

"What sources?"

"They also say you were pretty upset with him that night. You broke off your engagement and stormed out of the hospital room."

"Yes, I did."

"Because you found out about another affair?"

"That's none of your business." She glared at the heavyset detective.

"Is that why you killed him?"

Jasmine tsked at him with disgust. "I said I didn't kill him."

"All killers deny it." He loosened his gaudy tartan tie.

"I'm not a killer." She gritted her teeth.

"You had motive and access to all his personal items. Did you know we discovered he was being poisoned to death, bit by bit?"

"What?" Her chin quivered and a tear spilled down her sallow cheek. "Poisoned?"

"You are the one person he would have trusted most, and the one with the biggest reason to want him dead."

"In case you haven't checked all of your facts, Detective, there were a lot of people who were furious with Luther. But I for one, never wanted him dead."

"You had no idea he took you out of his will?" He slammed his palm down on the metal table, and she jumped.

"He never put me *in* his will. Jasper is supposed to be the sole beneficiary, and I've always been fine with that. I never stayed with Luther for his money."

"You sure had a fancy house and car, Miss Trudel."

"I also have a decent job, and every item I have is in my name. Luther asked me to move in when he bought the house." She steeled her back, sucked in a breath, and then exhaled as she settled against the metal chair and addressed him in a monotone voice. "I'm tired of these antics."

"You can't sit there and expect me to believe you didn't want to kill the cheating bastard."

"What I expect from you, Detective, is to give me my phone call."

A quick knock at the door interrupted their squabble

"Phillips, this interrogation is over." A middle-aged black woman opened the door and shot a stern glare toward Jasmine's tormenter.

"We just got started, chief."

"Well, you're finished. Her father-in-law is here. With a lawyer."

***

"HOW COULD they think Jasmine would ever hurt me? She's the gentlest woman I've ever met." Luther slammed the door after he entered the hotel room.

"Your temper is flaring."

"You're damn right it is. This shouldn't have happened to her." He paused and stood in the middle of the room. Luther pulled his shoulders back with revelation and spun around to look at Gabrielle. "*He* told the cops that Jazz broke up with me, didn't he?"

Gabrielle raised her brows and bit her bottom lip as she hesitated to answer.

"That prick. I could kill him for this." He wrung his hands, and his knuckles whitened.

"What do you plan to do about it?" Gabrielle took a seat in the chair and crossed one leg over the other. She folded her fingers together and cupped her bouncing knee.

"Plenty."

"Luther." She stood up and faced him. "You can't just march over to Marvin's and claim retribution."

"He's not gonna get away with this, any of it. I won't let her take the fall for my murder. Dad, Giselle, all their lives are screwed because of that asshole. I'm gonna make him pay for it."

"That is what I'm worried about."

"Look, I'm not gonna go all Rambo on him. I've got an idea."

"You already have one strike against you." Gabrielle crossed her arms over her chest and shot him a fierce glower.

"Believe me that I know. To get Marvin can't be a simple act of aggression. That prick deserves so much more thought and consideration.

"So then, what is the next part of your master plan?"

"First, I need a shower and a bite to eat. I need a clear head."

"You need to sleep. It's the end of day four."

"Fine, but I have stuff to take care of at first light."

"Such as?"

"First, I'll need a ride."

"I thought you weren't a fan of my way of transportation."

"It's an acquired taste, but I'll survive. Besides, this place, I need to get in unseen, and security won't let me through the door in this body."

***

"FOR THE record, this is a bad idea." Gabrielle stood to the side as Luther yanked the large framed beach themed oil canvas off the office wall and set it on the floor.

"I heard you the first twenty times." He placed his ear against the dial and started to twist. "Hey, angel, if you're so worried I'm gonna mess my chance up, don't you have some angelic power to make me stop, like maybe electrocute me, drop me down an elevator shaft, into a grave, or any other fun tricks?" He flashed a one-sided grin.

"No," she huffed. "We are not allowed to interfere with free will. That is why you're being tested, Luther. I can guide you, but it is your decision that will be judged, not mine."

"Understood. So, is it safe to assume you won't pull any more karma cards on me for my actions?"

"It is." She tucked her hands behind her back and leaned against the wall and let out a heavy sigh.

"It's gonna be okay, Gabby."

"Gabrielle, not Gabby. Not angel, my name is Gabrielle." She glared.

He shook his head with amusement. "Okay."

"You know the combination?"

"Not yet, but I'm pretty good at cracking safes." He winked at her and continued.

"Oh, more acquired skills from your past life, I see?"

"You could say that. Jewelry has never been an easy grab."

"Aw, right. You were a jewel thief too. How quaint." She put her hands on her hips and cocked her head.

"I just took the items I knew they wouldn't miss right away."

"Well, that makes it better, I suppose."

"Do you mind? I'm trying to concentrate here." One final click and he turned the handle, granting him access to the safe.

"I shouldn't be here with you doing this, Luther."

"It's okay, I've got this. You go do...I don't know, whatever archangels do. I'll call you when I need you."

Gabrielle shook her head with disapproval then vanished in a poof of flame.

"Well, well, well, old buddy, what have we got here?" He fished through the contents in the box.

Chapter Fifteen

FEET ON the desk, Luther waited for his target. He intertwined his fingers behind his head. The items on display in front of him, the phone set, everything was prepared for the big event.

"Twelve o'clock on the dot. He'll be in that door any minute as the regular Thursday meeting always ends on time for lunch." He glanced around the rest of the office and took in the minute details he had failed to notice when alive. The single personal item on display was a picture of Marvin and his wife, Beth, on his desk. No doubt, a stage prop for his future victims that painted him as the ideal husband. It sure fooled Luther all these years.

The devious smirk on the crafty little bastard's face caught his attention. Luther picked the photo up and studied it, then noticed a familiar item on Beth's hand she'd draped over his shoulder. Beth wore a heart-shaped emerald ring. Just like the one Jason told him about in the hospital after the accident. The one he spent all his money on to propose to Jasmine that fateful night.

"Son-of-a-bitch. You did do it. You took the ring after you set him up." This evidence reaffirmed any doubts he'd begun to have about his old friend. "You're going down."

At the blissful sound of the door handle turning, Luther fumbled with the items on the desk then rested back in the chair with his feet up, waiting in anticipation. Marvin waltzed in, oblivious to his presence until after he closed the door and tossed his briefcase onto the couch. As soon as he looked at Luther, he snapped.

"Who the hell are you?"

"You're worst nightmare, buddy."

"You have till the count of three to get your ass out of my office before I call security." He reached for the cell phone on his belt clip.

"Go ahead. While you're at it, you might wanna tell them Luther sent me."

"Luther? He's dead." His words were harsh and cold.

"I know. That's why I'm here. It's time to pay the piper."

"Who the hell are you, and how did you get in my office?"

"You can call me John. I'm a very good friend of Luther's, and I know every last detail of what you've been up to."

"You don't know shit." He sneered.

"You think so?" Luther brought his feet down, sat up straight, and rolled his sleeves. "You're a gambling man, or so I've heard." He fanned out envelops on the desktop, like dealing a deck of cards. "I'll see your three estates, a Rolex, and a BMW and raise you...hmmm, let's see...fifty to life for insider trading and fraud, and I'm sure we can name a lengthy list of other crap you've done."

"I don't know what you're talking about," he scoffed.

"Sounds like you have a little memory loss, bro. They have meds for that at the West Haven Sanatorium." He arched his brows, rested his arms on the desk, and smirked.

Marvin stood there with tapered eyes, staring at him. "Where?"

"Where I found Giselle, your mother. We can add impersonating a doctor to the pile." He pulled out one of the envelopes and tossed it onto the desk in front of him.

Wily and shrewd, more so than Luther had ever observed, Marvin picked it up, opened it, and glanced at the forged documents that implicated him and tossed them back to the pile of evidence. He turned and grabbed his briefcase from the couch, placed it on the desktop, and plunked himself into the chair on the opposing side of the bureau.

"I see where you're going with all this, pal."

"The name is John."

Marvin opened up the leather case and pulled out a checkbook.

"Alright, John. Cut the crap and tell me how much you want to keep quiet."

"I don't want your money, asshole."

"Don't be stupid, everyone wants money. Name your price."

"What I want is your head on a silver platter." Luther cracked his knuckles.

"You make it sound like this is personal for you."

"It's very personal, but what I'll settle for is you to make things right."

"I don't follow." He shrugged.

"For Jasper, Jasmine, Giselle, and even Beth."

"How do you propose I'm supposed to make things right?" He leaned back in his chair. "Not that you've told me what is wrong."

"For starters, you're gonna admit to me what you've done to each of them. Then, you're gonna give them all back the money you took, and maybe, just maybe, I won't send you to jail for murder."

"Murder? Who do you think I murdered?" He folded his arms across his chest and lifted his chin.

"Luther, for starters, and the near death of Jason Callahan in Mexico five years ago."

"You sound like you know some things. How can I be sure you aren't tapped with a wire?"

"I know everything. And...you don't. I'm not, but you're welcome to check me for one if that would make you feel better."

Luther stood up, lifted his shirt, and did a three-sixty.

"Are you a cop?"

"Hell no." He sat down again and fixed his shirt.

"How did you find out?"

"A little bird told me some stuff, and then there's all this evidence I found in your private safe."

"What evidence?"

"Forged legal documents which name you Luther's executor. They also name you as a psychiatrist when you committed your mother. Then there's the phony will, altered stock market reports, and a few other little ditties."

"What's keeping me from shooting a hole in your head and hiding all this evidence?" Marvin reached into his briefcase and pulled out a handgun, aimed it at Luther, and unlocked the safety.

"Plenty." He didn't flinch. "You have no idea how long I've been here, how many copies of every document I've made, phone calls, emails, texts I could have sent to protect myself. Come on, man. I know what a cold-hearted back-stabber you are. You killed your best friend and can't honestly think I'm stupid enough to not expect you wouldn't try and double-cross me."

"Fair enough. Let's say for arguments sake I believe you."

"So, how did you do it? How did you kill him?"

"Huh, I thought you knew the whole lot?" He squinted with a grin.

"More than you think."

"What now?"

"Well." Luther let out a heavy sigh. "I've put a lot of thought into that. First of all, I'd love one of those Cubans you stashed away in the safe. I must say you do have exceptional taste."

Marvin pulled his shoulders back with a sadistic smile. "Yeah, those are stellar, top of the line cigars. Sounds like a good idea to me." He clicked the safety back on and put the gun in his case.

Luther grabbed one in a clear tube from the pile of evidence on the desk, opened it, and bit off the tip. He picked up his trusty, old Zippo and lit the end of the cigar. Luther drew in a long inhale, held the stogie between his teeth, and exhaled a huge puff of smoke with a hint of amusement when Marvin dropped his shoulders and appeared to relax.

"I think you should join me, old friend." He took one of the cigars from the pile to hand to Marvin.

"If you don't mind, I've got one more to work on." Marvin leaned forward and opened the mahogany humidor box on the desk. He pulled out a half-smoked cigar and put it in his mouth.

"Sure, wouldn't want to waste them. Here, allow me." Luther held up the Zippo and recited, "Good times, buddy." He turned his head away as he flicked the flint.

When he'd turned back, Marvin's complexion had transformed to gray, like he'd seen a ghost. "That's what Luther...."

"So, tell me first of all about Luther's will."

Marvin held his cigar to the side while talked, and the smoke spiraled into the air. "It's all there in black and white. I've acquired a few skills over the years in how to draw up legal papers."

"So, you forged his signature and altered his will, naming yourself as his executor."

Marvin gave a slow, confirming nod.

"And, you evicted his dad and fiancée out of their homes."

"Well, his dad's house. Luther kept the deed in his safe, so I had easy access. All his papers were there."

"And your plan is to sell it all off and have some fun in the sun." Luther tossed the Caribbean brochure in front of him.

"It seemed like a decent place to hide out. International lines, no one could touch me."

"I didn't quite understand how you planned to get your wife's house."

"It is worth a pretty penny."

"But it's Beth's house. How would you get your hands on it, too?" Luther rested his elbow on the desk and his chin in his palm as he listened to the rest of his confession.

"I think I have that figured out, too. Partner?"

"What do you mean, partner?"

"Well, that house has been in her family for three generations. I didn't think it would be easy to get, but you've inspired me."

"How?"

"When we got married, we didn't sign a pre-nup. So, when she dies, it all goes to me. We don't have a kid. That's why I had a vasectomy in Mexico and didn't tell her. No one to get in my way of my inheriting her estate."

"How does a partner factor in to this?"

"Since I don't know you from Adam, but you seem to know a hell of a lot about me, I thought we could kill two birds with one stone."

"And by that you mean?"

"If you kill off the ball and chain, I will have an alibi, and this way, I can be assured you won't double-cross me and take the money for yourself. If you have blood on your hands, you'd have as much to lose as I would."

"How much are we talking here? This is one hell of a payload if you pull it off."

"Between Luther and Beth, I, uh...we can rake in about three billion dollars."

"Shit, you sure did have a global plan."

"Yeah, I'm that good." Marvin took a deep inhale of the cigar and released the cloud of smoke into the air, blowing rings.

Luther's chest pounded with adrenalin. "How long did it take you to set all this up?"

"That's the beauty of it. I didn't have any plans like this until after Luther had me nail that broke-ass artist in Mexico. He let me handle it, so I went large, and it felt damn good. Then I realized how easy it is to get people to trust you enough to milk them for every damn penny."

"Even your wife?"

"Icing on the cake. I married her for the money. I just thought I'd be stuck married to the bitch until old age kicked in. She's fifteen years older than me. Then, I got a taste of how easy it is to set people up."

"You sure did." Luther took another inhale.

"That's smooth, isn't it, buddy?" Marvin did the same.

"Sure is."

***

"SO, JOHN, it would seem, even you have your price." Marvin unbuttoned his coat and crossed one leg over the other. "How does forty percent sound to you?"

"I'm more of an equal rights kind of guy. Fifty-fifty and not a penny less. After all, we are talking conspiracy to commit murder."

Marvin puckered his lips with annoyance. "Fine, it's a deal."

"Maybe. Tell me one more little ditty before I agree to kill off your wife."

"What's that?" He draped one arm over the back of the chair and exhaled another lungful of thick smoke.

"Mexico, how did you do it?"

"Shit, that turned out to be so easy it almost took all the fun out of it."

"Go on."

"Luther wanted Jasmine. I could see why. What a luscious piece of ass."

Gritting his teeth, he fought back the urge to jump across the desk and throttle Marvin. He forced a half-wide smile. "You've got my attention."

"We overheard Jason when he paid the cabana boys to set up his special date when we were at the beach bar. Working class people are mighty poor, so some can be persuaded with a little incentive. I caught him on his way into the hotel and gave him five grand, American, to place the stuff around the hut."

"What stuff?"

"Some drugs, guns, and money. Easy to get if you know the right places to ask."

"Then?"

"I called the authorities and made an anonymous report of a drug runner about to make a huge deal in the cabana."

"What if Jasmine had been caught in the crossfire? Wouldn't Luther have been pissed?"

"He was always smooth with the ladies. I figured he would whisk her away before everything went down."

"Tell me about this ring?" Luther held the picture up, and Marvin's sadistic smile returned.

"Yeah, after they busted him, I paid a little visit to the Federales and made a...donation to their cause to make sure he never got out."

"I'd call that a little extreme."

"If Jasmine knew, Luther would have lost her, and I would have screwed up my chance to earn his trust. The pathetic loser had to go down to make my entire plan work."

"The ring?"

"I fished through his personal items at the jail and paid a little extra for them to give it to me. I told them the little shit stole it from me. I knew it would win me points with Beth. That's what I used to propose when we got back from Mexico."

"So, to sum it all up, you ripped off Luther, his dad, and Jazzy, you set up Jason, and you plan to kill your wife."

Marvin steeled his back. "You just called her Jazzy?"

"Uh...yeah, that's what Luther called her."

"Right." He shook his head and settled back into the seat. "Don't forget the good part, I killed Luther, too." He chortled.

"I thought he choked to death on Sandra Foley's ring?"

"Well, that was downright funny, but even if he hadn't, he would have been dead within the hour anyway." Marvin coughed, and perspiration enveloped his forehead. He took another drag of the cigar then set it in the ashtray on the table. With a shaky hand, he pulled a handkerchief out of his pocket and wiped away the sweat that began to drip down his temples.

"How did you plan to kill him?" Luther sat forward.

"I went to the hotel and put a note and a bottle of Dom Perignon on the cart, I knew Jacques would send him up some dinner. I laced the champagne with a lethal dose of arsenic." Marvin crouched over and gripped his stomach, groaning.

"But the police report stated they didn't find champagne at the crime scene."

Marvin eyed his private bathroom door and inched forward in his chair. "I stole a copy of the room key and waited outside. As soon as I heard him choke and drop to the floor, I snuck in, took the broken bottle and the letter, and got rid of them. I had to sweep up the glass." He held up his hand to show Luther three Band-Aids on his finger. "What a fuckin' mess. Dumb son-of-a-bitch's eyes were bulged out of his head. Funny as hell."

"Sounds hilarious." He flexed his jaw muscles.

"How did you know about Mexico?"

"I told you, I know everything."

Marvin patted his face and neck down. His shirt collar had become soaked with sweat. "I don't feel so good. I need the bathroom. Have we got a deal or what?"

"Let me think." Luther sucked in another mouthful of smoke, got up, and walked around the desk to sat on the edge in front of Marvin. He exhaled the cloud of smoke in his face.

"I don't think so...buddy."

"What?" Marvin coughed and dabbed his mouth with the saturated handkerchief.

"I have a message for you." Luther tossed another sealed envelope into Marvin's lap and waited for him to open and read it. In his own handwriting, he addressed a letter to his killer:

If you manage to survive the arsenic yourself, be prepared, you're going to jail for life.

"What the f—?"

"Like I said, I don't want your money, but I did want your head on a platter, and I would settle for you making everything right. Your confession is a start, which will get Jazzy off the hook for a murder she didn't commit."

"Confession? You aren't wearing a wire."

Luther dragged the phone base closer and turned it around to show the unwell Marvin. "I had you on speaker phone with 911. I had them muted, so you couldn't hear them, but they record all calls and have every word you said. Thanks...buddy."

"You should be the one sick right now." Marvin growled and dropped to the floor as he clenched his gut.

"Oh, you mean the cigars from the safe that you poisoned? The stash you fed Luther? The ones you planned to kill him with in a slow, painful death, day by day, with arsenic?"

"You knew?"

"I knew. That's why I switched them with the ones in your humidor. Just like you did with Luther. I figured you would keep your cigar free from poison. And for my own personal amusement, I dowsed your half-smoked cigar with the bottle of arsenic from the safe. Since I'm not well versed on how to poison someone, I can't be sure if it's a lethal dose or not." Luther offered an insincere pout. "Tough luck, Marvin."

"Uh," Marvin growled and retched violently.

"Oh, and just an F-Y-I, your wife is outside this door. No doubt she has heard every word you've said. Have fun explaining yourself out of this little ditty." Luther stood and called to Gabrielle.

"It's time." He unlocked and turned the knob, disappearing before Beth and the police barged into the room.

Chapter Sixteen

GABRIELLE transported them back to the hotel room and shoved at Luther's chest as she snarled, "You fool."

"I know."

"How could you? You were so close to redemption. You ruined your one chance with that stupid stunt."

"I know. I'm sorry."

Gabrielle slapped him across the face. "I'm right here, at your side. I have guided you, and you did what I counseled you not to do."

The iPhone vibrated in his pocket. Gabrielle's eyes widened with terror.

"I know." He hung his head and tapped the screen. "STRIKE TWO."

"I warned you not to take revenge. It is self-gratification, and it's your damned arrogance, stupidity, and —"

"You're right, Gabrielle. I'm sorry. But this is about more than me." He took her into his arms and stared down at her tear-filled eyes. "Hey, why are you crying? I thought you were the tough angel that kicks my ass?" He smiled.

She paused with her mouth hanging open. "Because, I...you," she stammered. "Because angels weep when we lose a human soul."

"Unless I'm mistaken," he said and placed his fingers under her chin, angling her head up to meet his gaze. "I don't smell brimstone in the air, and I don't see flames and the horns of Satan."

"This is no joke. I can't protect you from Metatron. I can't even shield you from yourself, you foolish idiot." She sobbed, and he held her close to his body. Gabrielle wrapped her arms around his neck and clung tight as he comforted her.

"Gabrielle," a curt voice called out.

Luther looked around. All of a sudden, they were back at the Great Hall, faced by two archangels who both wore horrendous scowls.

Gabrielle pulled back, away from his grasp, tucked her chin down, and her hands to her side like a scolded child.

"It's all my fault. She had no part in any of it," Luther protested.

"Enough!" Metatron's voice boomed throughout the hall.

"You will wait here with Jeremiel," he commanded Luther and snapped his fingers for Gabrielle to join him.

***

"METATRON, has it been so long that you forget the temptations of being a mortal? Mercy is not beneath you. Please, be patient and allow me to complete my mission. He is redeemable, I swear it." Gabrielle bent down on one knee and bowed.

"I have not seen sufficient evidence of that."

"He still has two days left to prove he can change."

"Are you in love with the human?"

She hesitated and stared at the ground. "I love all mankind."

"That's not what I asked."

"It would be a sin to love a mortal." She rose to her feet and turned her back to hide her tears.

"It wouldn't be your first time, I'm afraid." His voice softened and she spun around to face him.

"You speak of a very long time ago and a very different situation. It is not fair to compare the two."

"You have bent the rules and your orders to accommodate his arrogance and omnipotent ways."

"I guided him. Those were my orders, were they not?" She shot him a defiant glare.

"Mind your disdain for me."

Gabrielle inhaled and squinted hard. "Please, forgive me. I mean no insolence. I just wish to help this mortal redeem his soul, like I did for you."

"It would appear you wish for more than that."

She crossed her arms over her chest and gritted her teeth. "Am I removed from my duties or may I go?"

"Since when do you need my permission? You are a servant of God, not me."

"He is capable of deliverance. I know it."

"Come now, Gabrielle, you must see you are too close to him."

"All I see is that I've done the job I was allocated, and you stand in my way. Luther did a good deed at the accident, and you punished him for it."

"I made the determination that he broke the rules." Metatron turned from her, walked to a table with a large book, and sat down. He picked up a quill and busied himself scribing.

"Please, explain to me how you can hold him in contempt for other humans that took pictures he had no knowledge of. How can that denote him as breaking any rules? You made an unfair call, and you know it."

"He acquired fame because of it." He slammed his fist on the tabletop.

"Not by his own hand."

"The deed failed as a pay it forward notion the moment he—"

"Metatron," she pleaded. "Since when do you sit in judgment of who is entitled to God's forgiveness? He has been given his assignment. The expectations are clear and the timeline is set."

"I am aware of the parameters, Gabrielle. Your emotions cloud your purpose."

"My purpose has never been clearer. All humans face extenuating circumstances. Why would we not take into consideration forgiveness for a flaw, driven by unconditional love?"

Metraton snapped his head up and dropped the quill. "He has not completed the task of unconditional love."

"No? Then why, explain to me, would he risk eternal damnation to protect his loved ones?"

"Can you say," Metatron demanded as he stood up and faced her again with folded hands, "with all certainty, Luther's actions were of unconditional love and not revenge?"

Gabrielle remained silent.

"I didn't think so."

"Extenuating circumstances. Protection and revenge are often confused by humans, as you may well remember, Metraton. You, too, struggled with this motive before you earned your place at God's side."

"I did not poison a man for revenge." He glared.

"Luther knew well enough it was not a fatal dose. He made a stupid choice, but nonetheless, he made a conscious decision to ensure Marvin would live to see his peers prosecute him with fairness."

"Of this, you are certain?"

She dropped her arms to her sides and stood tall. "I am."

"Very well then, strike two will remain. However, I will permit him to continue. He has two days left, two tasks to complete, and two strikes against him."

"Thank you, Metatron."

"Don't thank me yet. His human nature is still strong. He can still be swayed to dark ways with little influence. There will be no other chances."

"Perhaps I failed at guiding him with this."

"The one failure I see on your part, Gabrielle, is that your infatuation with this human interferes with your ability to remain objective."

***

"I KNOW what you're thinking, Jeremiel." Luther approached the angel who stood with his back to him.

Occupied by books on the shelf, Jeremiel spoke in a soft voice. "I very much doubt that."

"You think that my actions are selfish."

"You were not brought here for judgment because of your philanthropy, Mister Evans."

"I really am trying. I couldn't let Jasmine go through that, not over me. She's a good person."

"She is an exemplar of goodwill and benevolence." Jeremiel turned around with a book, which rested in his palms. The pages fanned open until he nodded and they stopped.

"I never deserved her, did I?" Luther tilted his head back with exhaustion.

"No, you never did." Jeremiel placed the book in Luther's hands and sat down in a primitive fashioned wooden chair.

"What is this?"

"Her life records."

"You would let me see it?" Luther stared at the yellowed scriptures.

"I may not agree with your insistence to punish Marvin with poison, but I can see what would drive you so. Since you have at last opened your eyes to who she is, you should know who she had been meant to become."

"I don't understand."

"Read and you will." He pointed to the opposing chair.

Luther sat down and read through the endless pages of eye-opening truth.

"You robbed her of so much more than a romantic engagement that day."

"It says here, she should have finished medical school."

"Yes, her aptitude is incredible."

"But she dropped out a few years ago and became a medical assistant. She said school got too hard."

"Her academia, it would have been fine, but without the support of her partner, she didn't have the confidence in herself to complete it."

"And she was meant to develop...." He swallowed hard.

"She had many contributions to make to medical science, but she became side-railed when she spent all her energy in a vain attempt to fit into your world. She reduced her ambitions in hopes you would return even half the love she gave you."

"She would have had three children by now?"

"Yes, to become a mother, Jasmine has prayed for most of her life, and she carried an inherent knowledge that each of her children would be destined for greatness as well."

"And so as it is, she will be stuck, raising my kid in a town full of people who hated me."

"Precisely. The ramifications of your actions and betrayals will resonate in both their lives for decades to come and further define who they will be. Your son will have very little chance for success with these barriers."

"My son?" He glanced up as anticipation burgeoned. "It's a boy?"

"He would have been...."

Jeremiel's comment brought Luther to his feet with panic. "What do you mean?"

"The stress Jasmine has undergone, even prior to conception, did not create an ideal development for the child."

"Did she lose the baby?" His throat grew thick.

"She is still pregnant."

"When?"

"I am not at liberty to say."

"Can she be helped? Can the baby survive?" Luther dropped to his knees in front of the angel and clutched the book to his chest.

Jeremiel sat silent. His gaze fell to the floor.

"Please, don't punish her and the child—my child—because of my actions."

"It is not about punishment, Luther. This pregnancy was never meant to be."

"This is so much bigger than I ever imagined." Anger flooded him then a wave of sadness crashed down over him.

"Dear boy, the knowledge of the universe goes beyond the human realm of consciousness. Most mortals are so convinced their determinations in life will define every moment. They are too naïve to realize it has all been mapped out for them. The grand design has special plans for each and every one of them."

"Then why do you let us screw it up? Why can't you stop us and tell us how to get it right?" He hunched his shoulders.

"Free will is a universal law. We do not have the power or the right to interfere with it."

"So, when we get it all wrong, it messes up the whole blueprint?"

"In essence, no. But, as each person experiences their life, they either hold onto their faith, and with that, gain divine wisdom to further guide them. Or, in other cases, they lose their faith, therefore, they lose their way or path in life. They then must return in another existence to repeat the process until they get it right. For some, it can take many lifetimes."

"So, what about world hunger? War? Violence? If I'm here, being judged, what about the rest of the people that do terrible wrongs?"

"Everyone faces judgment, Luther. Not all at once, but in time it will be their turn to take responsibility for their choices. The global ailments and problems exist not just because of human nature but also as a part of the grand design."

"Our own personal hell on earth?"

"One could interpret it that way. But without challenges, how does one learn to rise above, to show compassion and empathy? To help fellow man, animals, and life forms?"

"It seems to me like the masses of people struggle and get punished so others can try to work at it."

"It is difficult to explain in words, however, understand this, each life form contributes with their own blueprint to follow. It all pieces together like a very intricate puzzle. The Akashic Records are the picture the puzzle is derived from, and how it will, in the end, fit together in completion."

"If I understand this, we are all a single piece of the puzzle and have to find our place in it."

"Yes."

"And for Jasmine, I altered her puzzle piece with my arrogance and selfish ways?"

"It is a relief to see your comprehension grow, Luther." Jeremiel nodded.

"How can I make things right?"

"Complete your assignment."

"I don't suppose you can tell me my next move?" He rubbed his aching temple with his forefinger.

"Other than the completion of your two final tasks in two days?"

"Which are?"

"To learn the value of self-sacrifice and experience unconditional love."

"Do they have to be in order?"

"In actual fact, no."

"I'll be honest, part of me hoped that when I got a strike for protecting Jasmine, it would have counted as self-sacrifice."

Jeremiel gave a soft chuckle. "I know you did. You were always a little too cerebral with your scheming. But the self-gratification you sought with revenge tainted your intention."

"If I hadn't punished him, I wouldn't have received the strike?"

"You've got it. To bring him to justice was acceptable. To cause him to reel in pain and vomit, not so much." Jeremiel patted his shoulder and motioned with his hand for Luther to rise from his knees. "I do believe this is the first time I've witnessed you almost pray since you were a child."

"This week has brought a lot of firsts for me." He glanced down at the book again. He shook his head with pressed lips.

"I promise, I will fix things for everyone."

Chapter Seventeen

"HOW MUCH trouble did you get in?" He stood hunched over at the rail of the waterway. A cloud of gloom permeated his brain.

"You don't need to concern yourself with me, Luther. I've been around a long time. I will be fine."

"I didn't thank you, though. For your help. I know you tried to encourage me to make better choices."

Gabrielle stepped back and studied his face.

"What?"

"Is that remorse I hear?"

"I don't wanna get into it."

"It is day six. Where do you plan to go next?"

He shrugged. The muscles in his face were too heavy to force a placating smile.

"You seem sad today." She leaned on the rail beside him and gazed out to the water.

"I guess I have some stuff on my mind. You know, like purgatory, the meaning of life...."

"You can still talk to me, Luther."

Hesitant, he inhaled a deep breath before he spoke. "How much do you know about what is about to happen?"

"They tell me what they feel I need to know."

"How much, Gabrielle?"

She dipped her chin down and shook her head.

"Any idea when it happens?"

"You can't stop it, Luther. Even if you were there."

"No, but I don't want her to go through it alone."

"Will this get us in trouble again?"

"Maybe." He glimpsed at her from the side.

"I knew you would be difficult to guide."

"So, how are you at following?"

She puckered her lips and crinkled her brows. "Not so good."

"Yeah, I figured as much." He nudged her shoulder with his. "Come on, there isn't much time to spare."

***

LUTHER knocked on the wooden door and sucked in a sharp breath when it opened. "Da— er, Jasper?"

"That's right." He strained his bright eyes against the sunlight coming from behind Luther.

"I'm John. A friend of Jasmine's." The words jabbed through his chest like a knife.

"Right, right. We met at the house. She's upstairs, had to unpack. Come on in, son."

Son? His heart sank. *I miss you so much, Dad. I'm so sorry I didn't appreciate you more.*

"Can I offer you a coffee?" Jasper closed the door behind Luther as he stepped into the large foyer.

"No, thank you, sir. I wanted to check in on how she is."

"Well, she doesn't look all that well. She's been pale and tired."

"Maybe I should take her to the doctor? To make sure the baby is okay."

"She told you?"

"Ah, no. I wouldn't say that. I kinda figured it out."

"Jasper, did I hear someone at the door?" Her sweet voice echoed down the stairwell.

"Yes, your friend...." He glanced to Luther with knitted brows.

"Uh, John, sir."

"Right." He turned toward the steps again. "Your friend John stopped by to pay you a visit."

"John?" she called out. Soft footsteps overhead were followed by a loud clunk and ended with a door closing. "I'll be right down."

"I didn't get a chance to thank you for your assistance with Jasmine and the move." Jasper held out his shaky hand.

Luther accepted and lingered in his grasp. "It was a privilege, sir. I'm glad I've been able to help."

His father stared into his eyes with his mouth open. "It's remarkable."

"What is?" Just like old times, his insightful gaze touched Luther's soul.

"I could swear we've met before."

"Uh...at the house." He pulled his hand back and averted his gaze in a vain attempt to avoid further interrogation.

"Not that. It's in your eyes...." He examined Luther for a long, awkward moment.

"John?" Jasmine's excitement captured his focus as she descended the long staircase. Clad in loose jeans and a sweater, she still appeared so frail. "I can't believe you're here. I just mentioned my guardian angel. Didn't I, Jasper?" She smiled. On the forth step down, Jasmine lost her footing and toppled over with an ear-piercing scream.

"No!" He rushed toward her, but she tumbled down the full staircase before he could reach her.

"Jasmine?" He and Jasper knelt down beside her listless body. Luther's heart pounded with ferocity.

"Oh dear, God. No!" Jasper cried.

"Jazzy, wake up. Please." Luther sobbed and reached for her."

"Don't move her." Jasper grabbed his hands. "There is a phone in the office through that door. Call 911. We don't know if she hurt her spine."

Frantic, he nodded in agreement and bolted to the office.

***

"HERE, SIR. I brought you a coffee. It's been a long wait."

Jasper accepted the cup and patted the empty chair beside him. Luther sat down.

"Two hours and they still haven't come out of surgery." Jasper's eyes welled up, and he muffled a whimper with the back of his empty hand.

"Da—" Luther's chest seared from his father's heartbreak. He rubbed his sternum, but refrained from any attempt to get away, despite the physical pain. "She's a strong lady. I know she'll be okay." He forced the words through clenched teeth.

Jasper sat silent and nodded. His withered cheeks had grown a pale shade of gray.

"Maybe I should go ask a nurse and try to get an update." He moved to the edge of his seat to escape.

His dad gripped Luther's free hand and stopped him on the spot. "Please, don't leave me alone."

His heart raced. "Not even for a minute. I promise."

"Thank you, son. I don't know how much more I can take." Jasper clutched his chest and gasped for air.

"You've been through a lot this week."

"More than you know."

"I know. I heard about your son." Luther rubbed Jasper's shoulder. "I'm so sorry about all you have had to go through, sir."

"She's having his baby." He blurted out and sniveled. "It's the last piece of Luther I will ever have. What will we do, if she doesn't...?" Luther's heart pounded. Although his chest stabbed with pain, he knew it was the empathic sensation from his father.

"Jasmine is gonna be okay."

"Mr. Evans?" a familiar voice sounded out with panic.

They both glanced at the doorway where Sarah, Jasper's maid and friend, headed toward them.

"I am so sorry, Mr. Evans."

Jasper leaned on his cane to stand up as she hugged him tight.

"Is there any word yet?" She looked to Luther as Jasper clung to her.

He shook his head. "If you will excuse me for a moment?"

She nodded and sat down, consoling Jasper.

***

LUTHER skulked down the desolate corridor and tried to peek through the tiny square window in the door. Several people in surgical scrubs and masks bustled around, obscuring his view. Unable to see much, except the thin blue sheet draped over Jasmine's legs on the table, he growled with impatience. There were half dozen machines all around her. Beeps, the whooshes of the air pump, and the constant chatter in the room were muffled by the closed door.

Helpless and afraid, he glanced around to search for any signs of what he should do next. A glimmer of color caught his eye, and he strolled farther down the hallway until he reached the origin of his distraction.

In front of the door, he stood and read the sign above and gave a slight smile. "Okay, I get it."

A blanket of sorrow and dampened acceptance shrouded him, and he pushed the door open. Passing the rows on his way to the front, he took a knee by the second pew and faced the altar. Luther folded his hands and bowed toward the stained glass image of Jesus.

"God, I know I'm out of practice, so bear with me. Please keep Jasmine safe and my dad, too. I'm so sorry for all the hurt I've caused everyone. I understand now, it's always been about so much more than me."

For the first time, in as many years as he could recall since his mother's death, the stillness swathed Luther with a minute sense of peace. He stayed there, engaged in silent prayer for what seemed to be a very long while.

"It's a relief to see someone else ask for help," a familiar voice sounded beside him. Luther opened his eyes to find his dad seated in the pew at his side. "I have found private worship has waned in young folks over my years."

"I didn't hear you...." His pulsed raced.

Jasper slapped him lightly him on the shoulder. "Son, it's of no mind to God if you're on your knees or sitting down. What matters is your intent." He patted the bench for Luther to join him.

"So, I've learned." He rested back into the squeaky wood seat as he caught the emptiness that filled his father's eyes. "She's gonna be okay. I promise."

Jasper nodded, and his attention drifted to the stained glass up high. Luther scanned the rest of the room and admired in the masses of flickering candles, painted portraits, and statues that filled the small chapel.

"My son was about your age," he said in a faint whisper.

"Yes, sir."

"Not many people understood him."

"But you did."

"I tried, but I'm not so sure I did." Defeat resonated in his words.

"Mr. Evans, this may sound strange coming from me... I mean, you don't know who I am...."

"I know you have kind heart. You've been so good to Jasmine these past few days. To show that kind of compassion to a stranger is rare."

"Thank you." Luther hung his head. "I believe your son treasured you." He swallowed hard. "But he didn't know how to say or show it when it mattered most."

"It sounds like you know a lot about a man you never met."

"I wonder if we are more alike than people would ever know." He treaded on dangerous ground and spoke with deliberation.

"In what sense?" His dad turned and faced him, his eyes brightened with curiosity.

"I've had some lessons of my own to understand that I should have a long time ago."

"Such as?"

Luther pondered the question for a moment and scrubbed his face with his palms. After he sucked in a deep breath, he continued. "Compassion, truth, and that the universe has a lot more to do with our little lives than I ever imagined."

"Sounds like you discovered faith."

"Somethin' like that." He grinned. "I lost my mom in an accident as a kid."

"We lost my Gladys the same way." Jasper chewed on his bottom lip.

"Yeah?" The empathic chest pain returned, and Luther rubbed his sternum. "Religion had always been such an important thing to both my parents, and when I look back, I guess I resented my dad for loving the God I believe took my mom away from me."

"Uncanny." Jasper nodded with an intense stare. "That's what my son said."

"For a long time, I spent my days pushing people I cared about away, and I did some shameful things. I guess I didn't want anyone else to get close enough to ever hurt me again." He slumped over. "I didn't realize my heart had turned to stone, and it never once occurred to me the damage I'd caused to so many people's lives."

"How did you get to become this fine young man?" Jasper pointed to him.

"Although it may seem a little late, it hit me how much I want to redeem myself. I wish I had been more like my dad."

"Tell me about him."

"My father," Luther said, his chin quivering and his chest tightening under Jasper's hopeful gaze, "is an amazing man." His eyes blurred with tears. "Dad loves unconditionally and loved me, no matter how badly I behaved, or how many people I hurt, and he blamed himself for my failures. He even tried to undo all the wrong I had done when I couldn't."

"Many fathers do, I suppose." Jasper grimaced and stared back at the glass.

"As it turns out, he's the one reason I want to be a better person. It's like, all of a sudden, these poison blinders fell off, and I can see life so much clearer than I have in years."

"That's wonderful, John." Jasper patted the back of his hand.

"I guess, what I want to say is that if I could change anything I've done with a snap of my fingers, it would be to take away all the anger that corrupted my judgment, the hurt, the disappointment, and the shame I caused my father." He tipped his head back with despair and sighed. "My dad didn't fail me. My own free will, my drive for self-preservation, that's how I screwed my life up."

"John, I'm sure your father wouldn't want you to be so hard on yourself."

"Maybe if I had been harder on myself all those years ago, things would have turned out different for everyone I love. I've made such a horrible mess for them all." He took Jasper's hand and looked him straight in the eye. "And I believe, sir, if he could sit here with you, those are the very words Luther would want to tell you himself. He would want you to know the truth, that he was scared, and angry, and if he could, he would take back every disappointment he ever caused you."

"You think so?" He arched his course gray brows.

"I know so."

"He didn't disappoint me."

"He didn't?"

"No, John. It made me sad, and I felt helpless that I could make it better for him."

Speechless, Luther sat still. How could he have misunderstood so much?

"I think if your father were to hear your words of confession, it would make him very proud of you."

"I hope so, sir. The fact that you were able to listen to me means more than I can ever tell you."

Uneasy about how much further he could push the moment, he faced Jasper. "Mr. Evans, thank you." He held his hand out. His dad glimpsed down and smiled, then pushed it away.

"I would have counted myself privileged to have had you for a son." Jasper hugged Luther tight.

"Mr. Evans?" Sarah peeked into the chapel and sighed with relief. "There you are. I got worried when you didn't come back from the men's room."

"Is there any word yet?" He used the back of the pew to pull himself to his feet and leaned on his cane.

"No, not yet." She waited at the door.

"I don't want to miss the doctor if he comes out with an update." Jasper gripped Luther's shoulder. "When all this settles, perhaps you can stop by the house for dinner? I know Jasmine will want to have you for a visit."

"Uh...." Panic filled him. "About that, sir." He looked to the floor to avoid his father's gaze. "I don't have much time left. I have to go away soon."

"Oh." He frowned. "That's a shame. We just got the chance to know you."

"Anyway, I'll be here for another day or two. I want to make sure she's okay."

Jasper flashed a gentle smile. "I'll let you know if we hear word."

"Thank you."

Chapter Eighteen

"GABRIELLE, I need you."

She appeared beside him at the surgery room door. "How can I help?" She rubbed his arm.

"Please, I just need to be in there, beside her. I'm so scared."

"I can't help unless you are in spirit."

"I'll take what I can get, please."

One moment he stood in the hall, the next Luther found himself inside the surgery room. He wandered around, scanned the machines, and took inventory of all the medical gadgets hooked up to her. Jasmine had a breathing tube taped to her mouth that flowed into her throat. The pump gushed with each expansion of air into her lungs. There were two monitors with heartbeats, one for her and the other—for the baby.

"He's still alive?"

Gabrielle stood beside him and held his hand as he watched with fleeting glances at the flashing lines.

"We need three more units of blood. She's still hemorrhaging," a lanky doctor barked at the nurse to his side, who fled through the door at his command.

"We're almost out. She has a rare blood type." A second nurse dabbed the perspiration of the surgeon's forehead.

"I'm not sure we can stop the bleeding in time," the heavy-set male surgeon who faced toward Luther, announced. "Nurse, I want you on the phone with the blood bank and surrounding hospitals. We need a stock of AB negative, stat."

"Yes, Doctor Hatfield." The curvy woman dashed out of the room.

"I need another sponge, hand me the clamp...." The demands were sharp and sporadic as a team of four worked on her abdomen under the crimson-drenched tented sheet.

"Jazzy?" Fear clawed at his stomach. Her skin had turned waxen, and her heartbeat irregular. The tinier, faster blips snared his attention.

Luther walked up to the monitor, the live ultrasound. The small strand of white pearls along the screen had become curled up and jagged compared to the perfect, smooth thread he'd seen only days ago. The tiny heartbeat started to slow, the rhythmic blips skipped and jumped, the sound lessened, and the movement on the screen stopped.

"We're losing it," the third masked doctor called out. She stepped through Luther's ethereal body and adjusted the dials. The flatline sound shrieked through his head.

"No," Luther whimpered. He reached for the display, and his hand sank through it.

"We have to stop the bleeding. Her trauma is too much. We can't repair the damage."

"We have to proceed with the hysterectomy, Dr. Spiel," another masked surgeon announced.

"Hysterectomy?" Luther blathered. "No, she's gonna have three kids. They can't do that to her!"

"If they don't, she will bleed to death."

"I have to help in some way. Please tell me I have a rare blood type in this body."

Gabrielle offered a soft smile. "I'm sure that's one favor we can grant."

"Thank you." Emptiness flooded him as she led him down the hall to donate blood.

***

JASPER lay curled up on the vacant hospital bed in the corner of the room, sound asleep. He whimpered from time to time between the occasional snores. Outside the window, the view of the sunset across the city landscape appeared muted by the enveloping fog.

At her side, as she lay asleep, Luther sat in the hard metal chair with his forehead rested against her hand, which he'd held for the last two hours.

A soft groan followed her gentle twitching of fingers in his grip.

"Jazzy?" He straightened his back and searched her face for signs of consciousness. "Baby, can you hear me?"

She tipped her head to the side in one clumsy drop and struggled to open her swollen lids.

"Baby, I'm right here with you. You're gonna be okay." He brushed her raven hair back from her cheek.

"Luther?" She babbled incoherently. "Luther, can we talk over dinner? I have to talk to you. It's important." She gripped the blanket over her stomach.

"Jazzy, I'm here, baby. I swear, I'm right here."

"It's the morphine," a voice called out from the door.

"What?"

A nurse entered the room with a stethoscope. "She's on a heavy dose of morphine for the pain. She won't be lucid for awhile, I'm afraid." She propped open Jasmine's eyes, inspected her pupils with a penlight then lifted her wrist and checked her pulse.

"It was touch and go for awhile there, but the doctor said she will pull through."

"Thank God," he blurted out then paused and glanced up at the ceiling with a half-wide smile. "Thank God." He grimaced at the nurse. "Can you please tell me why they had to do a hysterectomy? Did the fall down the stairs cause that much damage?"

"Did the doctor not come and speak with you gentlemen?"

"No, ma'am. You're the only one who's talked to me since they brought her into the room."

"I see." She stood at the bedside and faced Luther with sullen eyes. "The surgeon indicated on her chart she'd been bleeding internally prior to the fall."

"From what?"

"They found several fibroid tumors. They had to remove them all, that's why surgery took so long."

"Cancer?" His heart pummeled his chest.

"They have to wait for the biopsy results, but she had regular exams previous to surgery. These were new, unexpected, but her prognosis seems good."

"But, she'll never have children."

The nurse drew in a slow breath and primped Jasmine's pillows and tucked her blankets in. "Childbirth is no longer possible." She paused then glanced back at him with a frown. "I'm sorry, sir."

Speechless, he could only bob his head in response as he gripped Jasmine's cold hand.

"Her father should go home and get some proper rest." She nodded to Jasper in the corner.

"Miss, if it's okay, please let him stay. She is all he has. He can't bear to be alone until he knows she's all right."

The nurse offered a gentle smile then opened the cabinet, pulled out a thick hospital blanket, and covered Jasper.

"Thank you for your kindness."

***

"JOHN?" He awoke to her sweet voice as she raked her fingers through his hair.

"Jazzy, you're awake?" Relief rushed through him.

"What happened?" She clutched the blanket over her swollen tummy. "What...wait a minute. Where am I...?" Panic flooded her voice, and she swung her head back and forth as she scanned the room.

Luther shook his head and struggled to find the words. "You had an accident. You fell—"

"Down the stairs?" She gasped.

"I'm afraid so."

"My baby?" Her eyes glistened, and her lips quivered.

"I'm so sorry." He held her hand between both of his and squeezed tight. "They tried for hours to save him."

"Him?" She bolted upright, shrieked with agony, and dropped back onto her pillow.

"Honey, please, stay still."

"What's wrong with me?" She patted down her stomach. Her excruciating pain stabbed through his gut.

"Stop, just...hang on a sec." He gasped for breath through the empathic torture.

"What did they do to me? To my baby?" Bordering on hysterical, Jasmine writhed in her bed.

Luther jumped up, bent over her and held her pallid face between his palms. "Jazzy, stop and look at me, please. I need you to look at me."

Like magic, she stopped and stared at him with wide eyes. A wave of shock rushed through her and into him.

"You're gonna be okay. We will get through this, I promise you. You will not be alone—ever."

A single tear spilled down the side of her face.

"They did what they had to do to keep you safe. Jasper is right over there." He glanced over his shoulder to find his father awake and already at the side of the bed. Morbid fear filled his dad's face. "I promise you, it will to be okay."

"My baby," she whispered. "I lost him?"

"Jasmine, I'm here, sweetheart." Jasper approached the opposite side of the bed and sat beside her.

"Dad, I'm so sorry." She sobbed. "The baby was all we had left of him."

"It's not your fault. It was an accident. I'm just so thankful you're alive." He crouched over and held her tight as she wept.

Chapter Nineteen

"HEY, BUDDY, you look so much better since the last time I saw you." He entered the room with some helium balloons, wrapped flowers, and a get-well card.

"John? My hero. Hey brother, how ya been? I thought you disappeared on me." Jason sat up with a huge grin.

"It's been a busy week." He handed the balloons to Jason and dropped the bouquet on the end of the bed. "How's the pain?" He stepped back, hesitant to experience the burning yet again.

"Oh, so much better They're gonna get me skin grafts to repair some of the scars, but that will have to wait until I can sell a few paintings to cover the cost."

"Paintings, right. You're an artist."

"I told you that?" He dropped his mouth open.

"Yeah, you told me a few things, including how much you hate being under the influence of drugs." Luther winked at him.

"That's awkward. I wish I could remember." He glanced up to the ceiling. "What else did I tell you?"

"Don't stress. You didn't write me into your will. There's no reason to be embarrassed, I promise."

"Man, I'm going stir crazy in here." Jason wiggled in the bed. "A guy could go nuts just sitting around."

"I know it's past visiting hours and they're gonna kick me out when they see me, but do you think I could kidnap you for a small walk around the hospital?"

"I don't know. Am I allowed to get out of bed?"

"Hang on. Let's see what I can arrange." Luther dashed out of the room and down to the nurses' station. In minutes, he came back with a wheelchair.

"Alright, I can bust you out for a few minutes, but if you aren't back before the nurse's next round, I'm a dead man." He snickered to himself.

Luther helped Jason into the chair and draped a blanket over him.

"Wait a second." He studied his disheveled appearance. "This won't do at all."

"What?"

"Do you have any idea what kinda pick up joint hospitals can be?"

"No." He crinkled his brows.

Luther rummaged through the small drawer of the bedside table and pulled out a comb. He tidied up Jason's hair and straightened his hospital gown.

"Awesome." He grabbed the flowers and handed them to Jason. "Hang on to your bandages, we're bustin' loose."

"Not much of a ride, dude. I thought we were going for a walk."

"Yeah, well, another friend of mine took a spill, and she's checked into the room at the end of the hall. Here we are. I thought maybe we could say hi."

Luther wheeled Jason into the room and parked him beside the bed. He checked on his dad—sound asleep again. Jasper snored aloud in the corner bed.

"Jazzy, I got...."

With a heavy sigh, she shook her head before she opened her eyes. Jasmine licked her dry lips and fixed her gaze on Luther. "What?"

"Pretty lady, it's John." He coaxed her to awaken.

"John?" Perking up, she stared at him and blinked hard. "John." She smiled.

"This is my friend, Jason."

She dropped her head to the side, as though it weighed a ton, and struggled to focus on the face.

"Jasmine?" Jason whispered.

Luther took the flowers and showed them to her. "He brought you a gift."

"Flowers? How sweet."

Luther stepped back as she shook off her grogginess and stared at his new friend.

"Jasmine, is that really you?"

"Jason?"

Luther smiled.

***

HE STUMBLED into the hotel room and flopped on the bed, completely exhausted.

The vibration in his pocket didn't faze him.

"Luther, check your phone," Gabrielle whispered into his ear.

"Am I going to hell?" he slurred through the side of his mouth, his eyes sealed tight.

"Maybe," she goaded.

"What?" He pushed his body up from the mattress and turned over to drop onto his back.

"Then take me there, angel. I'm too tired to care."

"Aw, poor baby. Maybe I should just take the phone for you, then?"

She reached for it, and he grabbed her hand. "Don't even think about it. I can't afford to get excited with your hand in my pocket."

"Good point." She giggled. "Check it, or I will."

"Is that cheerfulness I hear in your voice?"

She hunched her shoulders up and smiled.

Luther pulled the phone out and tapped the screen. *Task five, completed.*

"Are you kidding me?" He bolted up. "I'm done?"

Gabrielle's joyful expression vanished.

"What?"

"You've completed the task to experience unconditional love in its purest form, but you've skipped a task, Luther. You still have one to complete."

"I did?" He dropped back onto the pillow. Grogginess enveloped his mind, and he drifted off to sleep.

***

WITH A LONG stretch, Luther struggled to wake. The sun beamed into the hotel room.

"What time is it?"

"It's ten o'clock."

"What day is it?" He sat up as panic consumed him.

"Day seven."

"I'm not finished, am I?" He let out a heavy sigh.

Frowning, Gabrielle shook her head. "I'm afraid not."

"I thought I'd gotten the hang of this. So what did I miss?"

"You got a task completed."

"Yeah, unconditional love. How did I manage do that?" He ran his fingers through his hair as he tried to fully wake himself.

"Well, on a global or specific level?"

"Is there a difference?"

"As a matter of fact, yes, there is." She sat beside him, collected his hand, and studied his fingers matched against hers.

"Do tell."

"For starters, the moment you stared at the baby's heartbeat and his ultrasound, tell me what you felt."

Luther sifted through his brain, dizzy from the plethora of emotions that encased him. "Fear, panic, shame, anger, doubt."

"I don't mean the trauma and grief. I'm talking about the connection." She placed his open hand between both of hers. The warmth resonated through his skin.

"I hadn't thought about it that way. The connection...." He searched for the words. "The first time I saw the baby's spine the other day, it seemed so strange, but cool. Last night, it was different."

"How?"

"This time, I thought, this is my son."

"Because you knew the sex?"

"Maybe...." He debated her question. "No, it was more than that. I was a part of creating him, the spine, the heartbeat." His smile echoed in his heart and soul, but then, a blackened wave of sadness crashed over him. "And then...." His chest tightened, and his throat grew thick.

"Then, you realized he died?"

"Yeah." Luther dropped back onto his pillow and folded his hands across his throbbing chest.

"But even though you knew the baby would not make it, you felt the connection, the love?"

"I guess I did," he whispered.

Gabrielle rested on her elbow next to him. He averted his gaze to the chair beside the bed.

"I know it hurts, but that's unconditional love, Luther. You allowed yourself to love him, despite the knowledge you would lose him. Even though you knew he wasn't meant to be in the first place. You mourn his loss, and you cherish those precious moments of knowing he was going to be yours."

Luther didn't say a word. The habitual urge to spew out bitterness had evaporated and only sadness remained, along with a deep contemplation about his capacity to love anyone.

"Chamuel had talked about how you pushed people away."

"Yeah, after Mom died, I didn't want to let anyone else in again."

"But you love your father?"

"That was different, I held on to anger and resentment for so long, I didn't pay attention to the love part."

"Because she died?"

"I renounced my faith in God. I was so pissed off and angry with the world."

"And your father?"

"I blamed him because he didn't agree with my need to be angry with God."

"You felt he should have been?"

"I did."

"And now?"

"I see how much time I've wasted over the years when I pushed him away. No kid expects their parents to outlive them. It never occurred to me...."

"That he would have to mourn you first?"

"Yeah, I guess. I felt if I stayed angry and distant, then when he died, I wouldn't be as heartbroken as when mom passed."

"Do you still feel that way?"

"No!" He turned to find her cherub face close to his. "I want more time. I don't want to let go. I missed out on so much with him."

"With many people, Luther."

"Yeah, that's for sure."

"And that is global. Your readiness to accept love from everyone in your life, your father, Jasmine, those were the bonds of love you allowed to heal in your soul. That is why you completed the task."

"How come I didn't get the self-sacrifice?"

"You expected to?"

"Well, yeah." He huffed with annoyance.

"Because you wheeled Jason into Jasmine's room and assumed they would pick up where you cut them off?"

Shame filled him, and he rolled on his side with his back to Gabrielle. "Yeah."

"That's not self-sacrifice, Luther."

"Says Metatron?"

"Says anyone."

"What the hell was it?"

"A convenient way to tie up loose ends in your mind, I'm afraid."

Over on the nightstand sat the iPhone. He picked it up, rolled onto his back beside her again, and tapped the screen.

"The battery power in this thing is incredible." He smirked.

"Very funny." She sat up. "What's next, chief?"

"More loose ends?"

"What does your phone say?"

"It says I missed a task." He grumbled and threw off the covers.

Chapter Twenty

FOR THE THIRD time, he rang the doorbell and grew impatient. Determined not to leave until he saw her, Luther waited.

Would you cut the poor woman some slack? Her life just fell apart. Gabrielle's voice filled his head.

I have to do this. He thought back to her in response. He pressed the button two more times then stepped back when someone pulled the small white curtain back from the side window and peered out.

"What do you want?" she called through the glass, seeming agitated.

"Beth, I know you don't know me. I'm a friend of... Luther's. Can I please speak with you for a moment?"

She disappeared from the window without a word. He let his shoulders down with a heavy sigh. Luther ran his fingers through his hair then turned to leave. The handle clicked, and she pulled the door open.

He spun around, surprised to find his ex partner's wife dressed in casual but preppy attire of a soft pink velour tracksuit and flawless make up.

"Who are you?"

"I'm a friend of Jasmine and Luther's."

"I'm sorry about his death." Her nostrils flared, and she stifled a whimper.

"May I come in for a minute and talk?"

"Of course." She stepped to the side as he entered.

A yappy white dog with long hair barreled down the stairs to her side and growled at Luther. "Kiki, stop that noise," she scolded and picked up the Maltese, nestling her to her side. Beth patted her long fur, ruffling the pink bow on her head.

"It's okay. She's keeping you safe. She's beautiful." Luther chuckled at the amusing recollection of how much Marvin hated the dog because it hated Marvin. "I'll bet she's a great judge of character."

"So I've come to learn in recent days." She kissed the puppy's head. "Would you care to join me? I have the kettle on for tea."

"Thank you, that would be great." Luther followed her down the massive hall to the kitchen.

"My maid, Stella, is in the laundry room. I suppose she didn't hear the doorbell, and I'm sorry if you had to wait long."

"Not at all."

He sat at the island as she poured the steaming water into the teapot and busied herself with a tray for milk and sugar.

"Please, don't go to any trouble for me."

"Nonsense. I've been without any companionship for a few days. Your visit is a pleasant surprise."

She carried the tray to the kitchen table. "Follow me."

"I wondered how dear Jasmine and Jasper are. Such a terrible loss for them both. They are such lovely people."

"Yes, it has been difficult, but they support each other."

"Jasper was always so wonderful to her. He is such a kind and gentle man."

Luther sipped the hot tea, uneasy about how to blurt out his purpose for the impromptu visit.

"Tell me—" She shook her head and arched her brows. "Oh dear, I've let a stranger into my home and never even asked your name." Her cheeks flooded with red.

"My name is John."

"John, what brings you here today? Is there any chance it has to do with my husband?" She gritted her teeth as she referenced the snake.

"As a matter of fact, yes." He placed his cup down. "I'm so sorry, Beth. I can't even imagine what you must be going through."

She nodded. "I wish I could say all that has unfolded came as a surprise to me."

"It didn't?"

"My darling, when you are married to someone, you see many sides of them, some they often choose not to show other people."

"Was there anything about his arrest that shocked you?"

"I'm not sure that the levity of all he has done has truly set in, just yet."

"I could understand that."

"Did he kill Luther?"

"Yes."

She slouched in her chair. "And he stole his house, and Jasper's?"

"He did."

"I was next on his hit list, you know."

"That's what I understand."

"I was in the office that day." She sat forward with a stern glare. "Outside the door, I listened to the whole conversation on his secretary's speaker phone." She hugged herself and rocked back and forth in the bistro chair.

"I didn't mean to upset you, Beth." The shaking of her limbs and stomach vibrated through him like they were his own chills.

"I haven't had a soul to talk to about it since it happened. I'm too ashamed to call Jasmine or Jasper, and I don't know how to reach Giselle, my mother-in-law. The ghastly things I heard he'd done to her, too." She shook her head, and her face contorted. "I have no family, no children. I am all alone."

"I'm so sorry."

"I can't imagine they would even want to hear from me. Jasmine and Jasper, that is."

"I doubt that, very much. They wouldn't blame you. You were a victim, just as much as they were."

"Should I call them?"

"Perhaps in a few days." The wave of grief that struck him was next to impossible to keep at bay. "She took a bad fall down the stairs yesterday."

"Oh, my Lord. Is she alright?"

"She will be in the hospital for some time. She needed emergency surgery." Careful not to share the whole tragedy, he needed to steer the conversation elsewhere.

"The poor dear." She winced and touched Luther's hand. "I wish I could help in some way."

"That's very kind of you."

"Excuse me, Mrs. Woodward?" A young, blonde lady stood at the entrance of the dining room.

"Yes, Stella?"

"My apologies, ma'am. I didn't realize you had company."

"Not at all, dear. What do you need?"

"This just arrived by courier from your lawyer's office." She approached and handed Beth a thick manila envelope.

"Wonderful, I have been waiting for this." She tore it open with clumsy fingers.

"Pardon me, John. I'm eager to complete these. It will take but a moment."

"Not at all." He sipped his tea.

"Stella, my purse is in the kitchen. Please fetch me my pen." The maid disappeared from the room. She returned just as quick and handed Beth a sapphire jewel-encrusted fountain pen.

"How long have you known them?" She spread the documents on the table and wrote on each page where neon pink *sign here* Post-it arrow flags indicated the space for signatures.

"A while." He grabbed his tea and took a long fortifying sip.

"Almost finished." She exhaled a breath, her shoulders let down a little more, and her face lit up with each page she completed. "I've re-done my will, in light of recent events."

"Given the circumstances, that's very wise."

"Some people," she said, glancing over her shoulder at the maid who stood at her side waiting and frowned, "believe I've lost my mind."

"You just endured horrible trauma, Beth. Cut yourself some slack."

The maid pressed her lips together and focused on the wall away from them.

"I appreciate the sentiment, John. I've never been more confident of any financial decision I've made in my entire life as I am at this very moment."

She completed her name with one final jab of the pen, folded the papers up, and tucked them inside the enclosed return envelope. "There, signed, sealed, and please be sure it is delivered immediately to the lawyer by courier."

"Very well, ma'am. They are still at the service door. It will be sent back with them." She nodded.

"And don't forget, my darling Stella, you have the rest of the day off. It has been a most challenging week for us all. Go tend to your family, my dear. Be sure to bring them the food and clothes I packed up yesterday. Mr. Woodward's belongings are all to go to the church for donation."

"Yes, ma'am."

"There is also a package in laundry room for you. Please wait until you are in the comfort of your home before you open it, that way I can be sure you will enjoy it."

"I promise, Mrs. Woodward." Stella's voice sounded shaky. She cupped her mouth and left in a hurry.

"That seemed to lift your spirits, but it threw her a little."

"I'll tell you a secret, my new friend," she whispered.

"Yes?" He leaned forward to listen.

"I am a firm believer in paying it forward. I have had a very privileged life, and I have been grateful for everything I've ever had."

"That's wonderful."

"With all that has manifested over the money that plagues me, I see no reason to keep it any longer."

"I don't understand."

"I'm giving every red cent to charity upon my death."

"That's a beautiful gesture."

"As I said earlier, I have no children. My family has died off over the years. What good is a large bank account that no one can access when there are so many in need?"

"I never thought of it like that before."

"To get back to our chat, John." She patted his hand with a perky smile. "John," she murmured and focused on the surface of the table for a moment in deep contemplation. "Your voice, your name...."

Luther's heart skipped a beat.

"It was...." Her jaw dropped open, and he grew anxious.

"I can explain." He held his hands up as if to surrender.

"You were the one in the office? With Marvin?"

"I swear to you...." He paused. "I just—"

"Saved my life."

"What?" He was stunned.

"You uncovered all those terrible secrets. You could have easily taken the money, but instead, you turned him into the police."

Speechless, he nodded, unsure of what would come next.

"Thank you." She grabbed his hand and kissed the back of it. "If it had been anyone else, they would have let him kill me."

"No, I'm sure anyone would have done the same, Beth."

"Being a woman of wealth, I can promise you no, most people would not have."

Guilt rolled through him at the thought of spoiling her joy for even a brief moment.

"What is it, dear?"

"I need to ask a favor of you."

"Of course."

"By chance, do you still have the ring Marvin proposed to you with?"

"As a matter of fact, that is one of the items I planned to have my lawyer sell off and donate."

"Oh, I see." He gripped his teacup.

"Tell me."

"The thing is, I know where he took it from...."

Chapter Twenty-One

"THE DAY IS soon to end, Luther." Gabrielle stood at his side as he clung to the doorframe of the hospital room.

"I know." He stood in awe, focused on Jasmine who lay partially elevated and awake in her bed. She stared at a magazine the candy strippers had left earlier that night.

"Why did you send me away for an hour?"

Luther winked and didn't say a word.

"I should know what you've been up to. How will I answer to Metatron?"

"It's cool. I asked Jeremiel to help me out with one last favor."

"Your time is almost up." Urgency filled her voice.

"I know." He held a finger to his lips and hushed her.

"Why are we here in spirit?" she growled.

"Because I just need to see. That's all I want." He beamed.

A jolt shot through his wraithlike body as the wheelchair entered the room.

"Hey, baby doll." Jason rolled up to her side and held her hand.

"I still can't believe you're here." Jasmine glowed at the sight of him.

"How crazy is this?"

"I enjoyed our visit last night." With a smile, she nuzzled against her pillow and stared at Jason.

"You fell asleep three times." He chuckled.

"I've never been one for drugs, I'm afraid." She held up her hand where the intravenous drip was taped in.

"I remember well."

"Where have you been all these years?"

He turned his head away from her, his smile twisted into a scowl.

"Jason?"

"We have plenty of time to catch up." He shifted and looked back at her with a grin. "Tell me how my girl feels."

"Numb," she half-laughed.

"There is so much I want to say and do. I don't even know where to start." He kissed the back of her hand.

Luther sidestepped the incoming group of people to the hospital room. "Ah, right on time."

First entered a flower delivery guy in a brown suit. He carried a long black box wrapped with a red ribbon and handed it to Jasmine.

"What is this?" She stared at him with amazement.

"I have no idea." Jason shook his head.

She untied the silk bow then took the top of the long, rectangular box off and gasped when she looked inside. "Roses? Jason, my favorites! You shouldn't have." She lifted the dozen burnt orange roses and took a long sniff.

"But I didn't—"

His faint words were cut off by the onslaught of music that reverberated in the room. A band of three mariachi players entered the doorway. They were in full traditional Mexican costumes of black with large red bow ties, jackets adorned with ornate gold embroidery, sequined trim, and tight-fitting pants with gold studs down the sides of the legs. They all wore large sombreros with wide brims. One played violin, the second a trumpet, and the third man, an acoustic guitar.

Followed by them was a waiter, who carried a tray with two glasses and a bottle of sangria.

"How did you do all this?" she called over the music.

Shrugging his shoulders, he held his palms up with confusion, "I swear, I didn't...."

A final man entered the room, in a black security type uniform. He carried a plastic delivery pouch. The man strolled up to Jason, with a stern expression, then pulled out of his package a sealed envelope first and presented it to him. He tore it open, and Jason read the hand-written letter to himself.

This never should have left your hands, buddy. I pray all the wrongs that were ever done to you will soon be made right. Don't ever let her go. Make her happy, and I will do my best to watch over you both. Here's to second chances.

Have a wonderful life together,

John.

Jason glanced up, his mouth hanging open, and accepted a little red velvet box the guard handed him. He opened it and stifled a whimper at the sight of the heart-shaped emerald ring that glimmered under the florescent lights.

"What is it?" she called out.

"Jasmine?" He sat stunned for a minute then struggled to stand up from his wheelchair and brushed away the tears that filled his eyes. He took slow, pain-filled steps toward her, and his chin quivered. The crowd of people stepped away, granting him access to sit beside her on the bed. Jason showed her the letter, and she read it.

She shrugged her shoulders and stared at him. "John? I don't understand."

Jason flexed his jaw and swallowed hard then opened the box and presented the long awaited ring.

"Jasmine Irene Trudel, I have loved you since the first moment I saw you. Every minute of every day, you are all I have thought about. When we were apart, my heart was empty, my life meaningless. Will you do me the divine honor of marrying me? I would be so blessed to spend the rest of my life with you."

Chapter Twenty-Two

BACK TO the hotel room, Luther sat on the edge of the bed and pulled off his restrictive leather shoes.

"That's it?"

"Yes ma'am. That's it." He dropped back onto the pillows with fatigue and an ear-to-ear grin, pleased with himself.

"Unless I've missed something, Luther; the phone did not ring." She stood in front of him and folded her arms over her chest with annoyance.

"No, Gabrielle. You didn't miss anything."

"So, you've given up?"

"No. I accept my fate."

"What?" she barked. "It's only ten o'clock. You still have two hours left to complete your final task." She grabbed his wrist and tried to yank him out of bed.

"Hey." He tugged against her grip and pulled her hard, so she landed on top of him.

"What the hell are you doing? Are you crazy?"

"About you." He brushed a rogue strand of copper hair back from her luminescent eyes.

"I don't understand." She pushed herself up and climbed out of the bed.

"This is supposed to be news to me?" He laughed.

"It's not funny. This is your soul, Luther. Have you not battled to redeem yourself for the last week?"

"I have." He sat up and raked his fingers through his hair.

"Why are you giving up?"

"I'm not. There are no more signs of where I'm supposed to go, what to do, who to save." He sighed. "Gabrielle, I'm exhausted."

"But...?"

"I wanted to say thank you."

"But I've failed you."

"You didn't fail. I did. You stood by me every step of the way." He snickered. "Well, almost. You did leave me alone for the hard stuff, like the flaming car, the paparazzi, the nuthouse...."

She clenched her teeth and shot him a fiery stare.

"Maybe I only had enough time to fix some of it, and maybe I did the best I could. But let's face it, five years of swindling, conniving, and hurting people. Seven days wasn't gonna cut it. But I'm okay with that. The people who needed me most, I had the chance to help. I can take that with me wherever I end up."

"You can't."

"It's okay. I got to tell my dad, even though he thinks I'm John, what I should have said while alive. He understood. I saw the peace it brought him when I explained in the chapel."

"That's not self-sacrifice. You can still do this."

"I've lived more of my humanity in the last week than I have in my entire, selfish, sad life. Jasmine and Jason have a second chance. Dad will never be alone because Jazzy wouldn't hear of it. Their lives can get better because I'm not in them anymore."

"I don't believe this," she snarled.

"I don't see any tears."

"What?"

Luther stood up and trailed his finger along the contour of her face. "From what I've heard, angels weep when they lose a human soul."

"Yes." She shook her head with frustration.

"Then, maybe I just need to have a little faith. If it's meant to be, I'll receive a sign or some infinite wisdom that will show me how to complete my last task."

"And what if that doesn't happen?"

"Then, I hope my divine angel won't get in too much trouble for a nice cuddle and watching a little television with me while I fall asleep."

"Excuse me? Why in Heaven's name would you want to watch television at this ungodly hour?"

Luther smiled and climbed back into bed. "Because, angel, I'm too tired to do anything else." He patted the bed beside him.

"Humans," she scoffed and stared at him with disgust.

"Yeah, I seem to get a lot lately." He tucked his hands behind his head and grinned at her.

With a huff, she took off her shoes, grabbed the remote from the television, and snuggled up beside him. "Fine, but no funny business."

"I wouldn't dream of it." He put his arm around her, and they nestled in while he trolled the channels.

Show after show, he clicked and clicked, unsatisfied with any choices.

"Maybe I expected too much for my final hours to at least have a decent show to watch," he joked.

He dropped the remote beside him then tangled his fingers in her long silky hair.

"We did have some serious heat between us, huh?" He kissed her forehead.

"You're talking blasphemy."

"Yeah, well, when you consider my track record, are you surprised?"

"Not in the least."

***

"A BREAKING story...." Out of the blue, the TV volume shot up to full and roused Luther from slipping into a deep sleep.

"What?" He jolted awake. Gabrielle slept in his arms, and the newscast glowed on the screen.

"Tonight, I'm standing here at the home of Mrs. Beth Woodward, wife of recently charged murderer, Marvin Woodward...."

"What?" Luther bolted out of bed and ran to the TV.

"Authorities have ruled her death a possible suicide, but it is still under investigation."

"Beth?" His stomach bottomed out, and he stumbled back.

"I suppose this is the sign you needed to finish?"

Confusion flooded him.

"I was just there."

"Yes, I realize that." Gabrielle took a seat in the chair beside the bed.

"Was she murdered? Did Marvin have her killed?"

"No, Luther. She was not murdered."

He dropped his face into his palms with defeat. "I was right there. I watched her give all her possessions away and was too blind to see it."

"It is understandable, Luther. You didn't know."

"Could I have stopped it?"

"No. The damage Marvin had done was irreversible in her mind, I'm afraid."

"I should have known. I should have stopped her."

"Luther?"

"It's not too late. I can fix this, right?"

"I'm sorry," she whispered with panic.

"No, too many people have died. Beth, my son. And Jasmine, Dad. They've been put through hell because of me. I need to make this right."

"I'm afraid you're out of time." Gabrielle pointed to the bedside digital clock. It read eleven fifty nine.

"You've gotta be kidding me!"

Chapter Twenty-Three

"LUTHER, are you asleep? Man, you're a cheap drunk, buddy."

A familiar voice roused him. A nudge to his side sent a jolt of surprise through him.

"Where am I?" He sprung his head up and looked around to find he rested against a long counter. In front of him were shelves of alcohol lined up, and a rack above him held dangling wine glasses. "A bar?" He scanned the room that seemed familiar.

"Come on, you can't be that drunk."

He glanced to his side to realize Marvin sat next to him with a cigar hanging out of his mouth. Classical guitar and trumpet music resonated throughout the room.

"What the f—?"

"Hey, you'd better get some coffee into you soon. That chick is not gonna swoon under slurred words and distillery breath." He chortled.

"You son-of-a-bitch, how the hell did you get out of jail?" Luther grabbed him by the collar and gritted his teeth.

"Excuse me? Did you get sunstroke?" Marvin eased back and plucked his fingers from his shirt.

Luther struggled for breath. He gasped and clutched his chest.

"Are you all right?" Marvin turned to face him.

"I can't breathe." Luther stood up and shoved back the leather stool.

"Are you hyperventilating? I didn't think you'd be so nervous to meet a chick."

A heat wave rushed through him. Luther dragged the back of his hand across his saturated forehead.

"Okay, slow down, buddy." Marvin gripped his shoulders. "Hey, barkeep, have you got a paper bag back there?"

Luther glanced around the room. It all appeared so familiar. Maracas and a vihuela guitar hung behind the bar, and a panoramic view along the waist-high walls revealed the brilliant blue of the vast ocean. There were patrons scattered throughout the place with margaritas and pitchers of beer and the savory aroma of nachos filled his nose.

"Is this the beach side bar?"

"Duh?"

"We're back in Mexico?" He spun around in disbelief.

"What do you mean back, buddy? It's our second day here."

"What day is it?"

"Wednesday."

"The date?" he demanded.

"Huh?"

Farther down the bar, Luther spotted a newspaper in the hands of a man in dress pants and a white collared shirt.

"Excuse me." He bolted over, grabbed the paper, and trolled for the date.

"Hey," the man snarled.

At the top corner, he read it and reeled back. "May 31st, 2009?"

"Excuse me, sir? I'm not done with that yet." The stranger glared.

"Sorry, pardon me." He handed it to the man and stumbled back, frantically searching his surroundings, unable to get a grip.

"Luther?"

"What time is it?" He glanced down at his bare arm.

"Dude, you're freaking me out."

"Time?" he snapped at Marvin.

"It's four-thirty. She'll be at the front desk right at five, like we planned."

"Planned? Shit, it's about happen?"

"Come on, stop playing around." Marvin chuckled and slapped him on the shoulder.

"I've gotta stop this." Luther barreled out the bar and toppled over on the sandy beach. Without hesitation, he jumped up and headed for the cabana.

A mile down the beach, he panted for air. He finally reached the small structure and found a cabana boy setting up dinner for two.

"Where are they?"

"*No hablo inglés, señor.*" The young man didn't quite look twenty years old, with his thick black hair slicked back into a ponytail. He held his palms up, seeming confused.

"Where is it? Where did you hide it all?" Luther ran inside and began to rummage through the hut. He searched for the condemning evidence. "*¿Dónde está ello? ¿Dónde escondió usted todo esto?*" He barged in front of the lad.

The bronze skinned man backed out, with wide eyes, and spouted wildly in Spanish. "*Usted es loco!*" He took off down the beach.

"Where the hell did they hide it? I have to stop this!" Luther threw his hands up in the air. "Please, I don't know what to do!"

Frenzied, he tore through every square inch and found no money, drugs, or guns. "Maybe...I dreamed it all?"

"No, Luther, I'm afraid you did not." Gabrielle stood at the entrance, clad in her wings and angelic attire. She held the jewel-encrusted goblet of love.

"Gabrielle?" He dropped onto his knees with exhaustion. "I don't know what I'm supposed to do."

"With this, I cannot help you."

Luther scrubbed his face with his hands. "Think, dammit, think." He glanced back up to her. "Is the stuff here?"

She raised one brow in response but remained silent.

"If I can, I have to change what happens."

"Listen to the divine wisdom in your heart." She disappeared in a flash of fire.

Luther clasped his hands together, closed his eyes, and bowed his head. "Please, help me. I don't know what to do."

In a moment of complete silence, the distant squawking of seagulls caught his attention. He got up, walked out to the beach, and approached the shoreline. He stood at the edge. The crashing tide rolled over his leather shoes and filled them with cold water. Each row of waves swelled as the sloshing of the water amplified.

A speedboat raced by that snagged his attention to the vast body of water. He followed the horizon back west toward the resort and discovered a long white boat at the dock.

"The cruise?" Revelation charged through him, and he patted down his pockets in search of the answer. He pulled his wallet out of his back pocket and fished through it, finding the two tickets he had purchased to steal Jasmine away that fateful afternoon.

"What the hell happened here?" an angry voice echoed across the beach.

Luther spun around to find a familiar person at the cabana entrance. "Oh, my God."

A second person at his side flailed his arms and jabbered loud and frantic in Spanish.

"It's ruined? It's all ruined?"

Luther ran back to the hut and went through the door. "Jason?" His stomach dropped.

"Who the hell are you? And why did you trash the place? I had such a special night planned." Helplessness filled his eyes, his jaw muscles flexed, and his temples pulsated. "I don't understand what this guy is yelling at me." He waved his shaking hand at the hysterical cabana boy.

"Look, I'm so sorry. There was a big misunderstanding." Luther approached the young lad and pulled out a wad of cash and handed it to him. "*Por favor, tome a mi amigo, y su muchacha al crucero de barco, en seguida.*"

The conspirator stared down at the substantial tip of two thousand American dollars then back to Luther with tapered eyes.

"*Hubo un cambio de proyectos.*" He looked to Jason and then translated. "There has been a change in plans."

"What's going on?" Jason demanded.

"Sir, on behalf of the resort, please, accept my deepest apologies. It came to our attention there were some dangerous individuals who planned to crash the cabana tonight. Once we heard tell of it, we contacted the authorities. They will be here any minute, and I sincerely wish to get you out of here to prevent any confusion about the matter."

"Excuse me?"

"In my experience, the Federales are less than understanding when it comes to illegal drugs and weapons. These individuals will be arrested and dealt with, but the legal system here is very different than that of the USA. Anyone caught on site will be arrested and persecuted, regardless of their innocence. Please, we don't have much time."

Luther approached Jason and pulled out his wallet, plucking salvation from the fold. "These are two very extravagant dinner cruise tickets for this evening. I realize it doesn't make up for this terrible inconvenience, but I pray you take them and use them tonight to avoid getting caught in the crossfire."

"I don't know what to say." Jason held the tickets with shaky fingers and tucked his chin to his chest.

"Sir, if I may?" Luther approached him.

"What?"

"Do you still have the ring?"

"How did you know about that?" His jaw dropped.

"Pardon me, I meant no intrusion, but earlier yesterday, when you were at the front desk with the concierge, I overheard you making arrangements for tonight."

"Who are you?"

"No one of consequence." Luther let his shoulders down and fought the thrumming of anxiety behind his right ear. "I wish you the best of luck. Jasmine is a wonderful lady, and I know you two will be very happy together."

"How do you know Jasmine?" Jason stepped back and narrowed his eyes.

"I bumped into her in the hotel lobby. She is absolutely sensational. I saw you two together later in the bar, and...." Confession time. "It struck me, how fortunate you were to have her. I wished I was so lucky."

Jason's face turned a surprising shade of white as he pulled a small velvet box out of his pant pocket. He held it open and showed Luther. "I have no idea who you are."

"A friend, Jason. And one who needs you to go before it's too late." His heart raced. "The cruise leaves in twenty minutes." He nodded to the cabana boy. "*Ver que él es guardado seguro, y no le convertiré en las autoridades para establecerlo.*"

"What did you say to him?" Jason tucked the box back into his pocket.

"I told him he better make sure to keep you safe."

"Jason?" Her tender voice sang in Luther's ears.

"Jazzy?" He rushed at her and hugged her tight.

"Excuse me." She pulled back from his embrace. "Do I know you?"

His heart sank. "No, ma'am. I must have mistaken you for someone else."

"Jason." She brushed past Luther in a panic. "What happened?"

He glanced to Luther for an answer.

"He, uh, has different plans for the evening, ma'am. This place was not what he signed up for, so we upgraded your dinner reservations."

Letting her go, without even so much as a kiss goodbye, was the hardest thing he had done this week.

Luther stood in the sand and watched as Jason and Jasmine strolled down the beach, hand-in-hand, following the employee to safety.

***

THE SUN SANK low over the water, streams of oranges, pinks and purples painting the sky. Luther picked up a strewn chair, set it at the doorway of the cabana, and took a seat. He patted his shirt pocket, finding a clear tube with a Cuban cigar and his trusty Zippo lighter.

He bit off the tip, spit it out to the side of him, and lit it up. He drew in a long, sweet musky lungful of smoke, savored the warmth and flavor then released it into the air. The rolling waves of the water grew loud and mesmerizing. As he waited for the inevitable, peace washed over him. No matter what, at least he could take solace he changed the fate of Jasmine and Jason.

The moment of serenity shattered at the distant screeching of sirens that grew louder as they drew near. Frantic flashing lights glowed against the contrast of the darkening sky. Four SUV's rolled up with a dozen Mexican police in full armor, baring rifles. They yelled Spanish threats, waved their guns toward him, and motioned to have him come out.

As he sucked in a sharp breath, Luther put his hands in the air, stood up, and took slow, cautious steps toward the arsenal. He dropped to his knees in the sand, put his hands on his head, and didn't resist. Luther let the cigar fall onto the ground from his mouth.

One particularly hostile officer ran up to him, screaming, then smashed the butt of the gun into his face with brutal force. Luther fell over and held his mouth; searing pain followed the warm gush of blood that spewed from his split lip. Sharp, countless wallops to his face and stomach from the combat boots of the officer only ended with a shrill voice that hollered in Spanish as two other police pulled him off Luther. When he curled into the fetal position and tried to fend off the sadistic assault, the man broke free from their grip and smashed Luther about the head and back.Fading in and out of consciousness, Luther remained face down on the beach, his hands tied behind his back. The copper-like taste of blood filled his mouth. He coughed and spewed crimson liquid onto the beige grains of sand.

***

"LUTHER? I'm here." The soft voice filled his throbbing head.

"Gabrielle?"

"Yes, I'm right beside you."

"Where am I?" He tried to roll over to face her, and a piercing spasm shot through his chest and side. The pressure of his lids stung sharply as he tried to force them open. He groaned in agony.

"Ssshh, you're in jail." The soothing heat of her touch trailed over his chest. She picked up his weakened hand and placed it between both of hers.

"They can't see you?" Panic rose.

"No, just you can."

"Why are you here?"

"I couldn't leave you here alone like this."

"What did they do to me?"

"You've got several broken ribs, cuts, and...."

"What else?" Taking mental inventory, every inch of his body wracked with pain.

"They hurt you terribly, I'm afraid."

"How bad is it? I can't see."

"You have internal bleeding, a concussion, and your face is...."

"How bad?"

"Broken nose, your lip.... If you survive, if they get you medical treatment, you will be scarred for life."

"So, what you're saying is my days as a lady's man are over?" He half-laughed then reeled with white-hot pain in his chest.

"Only you would make light of life or death, Luther." Her voice quaked, and she sniffed through a whimper.

"Wait a minute. Why am I still here?" He squeezed her hand.

"They pulled the man off you. He almost shot you in the head."

"Would have been a mercy-killing from how I feel. What I mean is, I ran out of time. Shouldn't I be in purgatory?"

"They are still deliberating your fate."

"Not much for their timelines, are they?"

"Luther, are you able to reach into your pocket?"

"Why, you got a hidden set of keys to break me outta here?" He snickered and wrenched with the pain again.

"Please."

Luther moved his hand with caution. Every muscle in his body ached, even his fingers hurt.

"How in heaven's name can my fingers hurt?" he scoffed.

"The bruising is all over your body. You're swollen up like a puffer fish."

"That's attractive, isn't it, angel?" He sucked in a long breath and exhaled through the discomfort. "I can't open my eyes." He tugged the iPhone out of his pocket and brought it up to his chin. "How am I supposed to read it? It's ringing."

"Would you like me to read it for you?" She drew in a long, shaky inhale.

"Please, sweetheart. I would like that very much." Luther reached his arm out, searching for where her voice emanated, and managed to grab a handful of long hair. He smoothed the lock with his fingers, cherishing the silkiness.

"Task four, Luther, is completed."

"What does that mean?" His throat grew thick.

"It means you had a stay of execution. You completed all five tasks with just two strikes."

"But not within the seven days?"

"That is what they are reviewing."

"How did I end up here when I ran out of time?"

"Jeremiel advocated for you to have a final chance to prove your redemption. He believed you earned it."

"So, he doesn't hate me? What about Metatron?"

"Not at all. I think, dear Luther, you surprised them—or rather us. You astonished everyone with your ability to redeem yourself."

"He didn't surprise me in the least." Another voice entered the room.

Luther's heart pummeled at the familiar sound.

"May I sit with my son, Gabrielle?"

"Of course, as you wish, Gladys." The warmth of the archangel disappeared as she got up from her seat. "I will come back after you both have some time to catch up."

"Mom?" His eyes pricked, and his chin quivered as she sat next to him.

"Yes, baby, it's me. I'm right here with you, just like I've always been."

Speechless, he whimpered and tried to sit up. Gladys gently pulled his shoulders and propped him up into her embrace.

"I am so very proud of you, my darling boy. I knew this was the man you were meant to be."

"I'm so sorry I messed up before." He gnashed his teeth.

"But, Luther, you made it all right again."

"Beth? Where is Beth?"

"She is alive and well. Likely at her bridge club as we speak."

Relief washed over him.

"Jasmine?"

"She is perfectly fine. Engaged and very happy."

"The hysterectomy?"

"Never happened. It's five years before your last memories of your life, darling."

"Nothing happened? No baby? No poison? Jason is safe?"

"Yes. With the final chance you were given, you managed to change the last five years with that one fateful night."

Luther dropped back onto the bed with an excruciating thud. "Thank God."

"By the way, you know I never learned to speak to speak Spanish. What did you say to the cabana boy to make him do as you told him?"

"Ha." He tensed against the pain. "I told him to please take my friend and his girl to the boat cruise right away. See that he is kept safe, and I won't turn you into the authorities for setting him up."

"That explains how fast he rushed them to the boat. Poor Jasmine nearly lost her shoe. He wouldn't let them stop."

"You just reminded me of where I get my humor from, Mom." Fearful of the repercussions, he held back another laugh.

A long moment of silence was filled with the bliss of his mother, holding his hand as she ran her gentle fingers through his hair. "Do you recall, Luther, how I used to settle you at bedtime?"

"I do." He smiled. "You read long Bible stories and played with my hair."

"I have noticed over the years in my absence, whenever you feel tense, you do the same thing. You brush your fingers back through your hair."

"It never occurred to me. I guess it comforted me."

"Most of your actions were self-soothing, my dear. I suppose, other than this, you will need to develop better coping skills."

"That's if they don't send me to purgatory, Mom. They haven't decided what to do with me, yet."

"If they let you pass and redemption is yours, what would you ask them for, Luther?"

He shook his throbbing head. "That's a tough call. I want to be with you," he sobbed. "But I also want a chance to do things right, Mom. I never wanna be that heartless guy again."

"I believe you, son."

The physical pain weakened under the tender aching of his heart. "I missed so much with Dad. I should have been there for him after we lost you. He's been so strong, but so alone."

"That is another matter I wanted to discuss with you."

"You do?"

"Yes. Jasper, your father always loved me, and will for eternity. He never even considered...." Gladys stroked the side of Luther's face with a tender hand. "Depending, on their decision, Luther, I have a very big favor to ask of you."

"Anything. I love you so much." He pulled her hand from his head and kissed it between whimpers. "I'm so grateful I had the chance to tell you." He covered his face with his other hand as he blathered.

Chapter Twenty-Four

A STREAM of sunlight penetrated his tender eyelids. "Jasmine, turn the—"

He bolted up, and stabbing pain shot out across his torso. "Son-of-a...." He groaned and eased back onto the wafer-thin pillow.

A hollow tin clanking noise startled Luther.

"*Usted tiene a un invitado.*" An officer dragged a metal cup across the thick metal bars, making a horrible racket.

"I have a visitor?" Luther forced his heavy lids open, but could only get them halfway apart from the swelling.

"Who is it?" He stared at the tall, gangly, uniformed man to find a scowl filled his contorted, tanned face. "*¿Quién es ello?*" Luther repeated, this time in Spanish.

"*No soy su secretario, le pregunto usted mismo, el gringo.*" He snarled and walked away.

"Yeah, that's fine, pal. I know you're not my secretary. You could use a lesson in civility, though." He massaged his tender side.

"Hey, loser. How does it feel to be on the wrong end of screw you?" His antagonist leaned against the wall, taunting him, as Luther sat up on the hard bunk.

"Who the hell are you talking to, you asshole?" Just to stand up was a feat in itself, but Luther fought against the shooting pain and hobbled over to the bars to face him.

"What? Luther? How the hell did you get in here?" Marvin's eyes widened, and he gripped the bars.

"Someone set me up. Any idea who, asshole?"

"Man, I swear, it wasn't supposed to be you." Marvin rubbed his forehead and paced back and forth in a frenzy. "I gotta get you outta here."

"That's gonna be tough, considering you set up thousands of dollars in cash, drugs, and weapons. Not to mention the extra you paid the police to keep me in here and deny me any phone calls. Ever!"

"I didn't...." He stopped and faced Luther. "How the hell did you find out? Why are you here? It was supposed to be that loser, and you were supposed to be on the cruise with that luscious piece of ass." He gripped the bars again, watching Luther with fright.

"Buddy, you did all this for me?" Luther stepped closer to him, with a placating tone.

"I did, I swear. I just...."

Luther stood face-to-face with his former friend. "Tried to make me happy?"

"Yes."

He aimed between the bars and punched Marvin right in the mouth, who then coiled back and held his face. Luther split his lip with one shot.

"What the fuck was that for? I said I'm sorry. It's all a big a mistake. It wasn't supposed to be you."

"Setting up a low-life loser so I could get the girl and you could earn my trust, right?"

"Yes." He shook his head. "I mean, no. It...." He pulled out a handkerchief from his pocket and dabbed at his bloody mouth with a shaky hand.

"A shitty way to win me over, *buddy*." Luther sneered. "Do you have any idea how many lives you fucked up with your lies and schemes? You are one evil son-of-a-bitch."

"What the hell are you talking about?"

"You wanted to make sure Jason would never get out of here and Jasmine would never find out what happened. All to keep in my good graces."

Silent and stunned, Marvin stared at him.

"The thing is, that guy you so tried to destroy never did anything to deserve this." Luther waved over his own battered body.

"You're hurt bad. We have to get you out of here."

"I don't want a fucking thing from you. Not now. Not ever."

"I didn't mean for this to happen to you, Luther. I swear I'll fix this."

"I would rather rot in this cell until the day I die than ever accept a single ounce of help from you. I know about you, Marvin. I know your plans. I know what you'll do to Beth. I know you just had a vasectomy and you plan to pop the question when you get back in four days."

Marvin shook his head with disbelief. "How could you know?"

"You plan to marry her. She's older. You hope she's gonna die off in a few short years and leave you her billions. You made sure she'll never have kids with you, so there are no heirs in the way of your big payload."

"I haven't told anyone."

"I know everything, and you're not gonna get away with it, again."

"Again?"

"Yeah, like maybe you'll plot my murder by poisoning the cigars you keep me well stocked with. Maybe with arsenic? Maybe, while you're at it, you'll forge legal documents and steal my house, my car, my money, and my dad's house, too. And maybe you'll evict him and Jazzy. Maybe you'll screw everyone over to make your fortune and jet off to the Caribbean."

"Or maybe they hit you harder in the head than you think. Where the hell is all this coming from, and why do you care about me and Beth?"

"It's coming from my conscience, and Beth is a kind woman. She doesn't deserve to get scammed by a slime bag like you. I don't ever want to be associated with you again."

"Fine." Marvin nodded emphatically, tucked the cloth away, and licked his bloody lip. "Fine, then perhaps you should just stay here and the hell out of my way." He glowered at Luther. "Good luck getting outta here. Like you said, I made sure you won't be getting any phone calls." Marvin stormed down the hall and left.

A familiar vibration sounded behind him on the bed. "Don't be so sure about that." He picked up the iPhone and tapped the screen.

Chapter Twenty-Five

LUTHER twisted his leather office chair to the side and faced his vast window. He cherished the brilliance of the cerulean sky for a moment and then examined the New York stock market section. He trolled down the columns of promising numbers.

"Excuse me, Mr. Evans?" The speaker on his desk phone sounded.

He spun around and tapped the phone. "Yes, Giselle?"

"Zachary Smith from the Department of Justice is on line one for you. He says it's urgent."

"Thank you." Luther picked up the handset and clicked line one. "Zack, how are you?"

He listened as he took notes.

"Yes, I've had that broker under surveillance for six months. It appears his assets have multiplied, considering his clients have been losing money. I filed my report with Joseph over at the Securities and Commodities Fraud Task Force a few days ago. He's working on a warrant for all client files, personal and business computers. They'll have him in jail for embezzlement by the end of the week."

"Excuse me, Mr. Evans," Giselle spoke through the intercom again.

"Yes?"

"I'm sorry for the interruption, but Mount Sinai Medical Centre is on line two."

"What do they want?"

"I'm so sorry, sir. They want to speak to you about your father."

Luther's heart raced. "Zack, I have a family emergency. I'll have to call you back later."

Tears pricked at his eyes, and he answered the call.

***

"PARDON me, my name is Luther Evans. Dr. Callahan called me in. It's about my dad, Jasper Evans." He stood at the information desk and tapped his fingers on the counter as he waited for the nurse to pull up the information on the computer.

"Yes sir. Your father is in the cardiac unit. Take the elevator up to the fourth floor, and someone at the nurses' station can direct you to his room."

After a long dread-filled wait, the nurse returned to her station.

"Can I see him, please?"

"Dr. Callahan is completing her assessment. She advised she will come and speak to you in a moment."

"Thank you." He stepped back then paced the long stark hall as the agonizing minutes dragged on.

"Mr. Evans?" a sweet voice sang out.

Luther spun around, and a lightning bolt of surprise struck him. "Jazzy?"

"Excuse me?"

The white lab coat and stethoscope suited her. "Forgive me, I must have confused...." He stared at her with amazement, Miss Jasmine Trudel. "Wait. Are you Dr. Callahan?"

"Yes, I am the head of the Cardiology Department." She approached and held out her hand to shake then paused. "Have we met before?"

"No!" He choked. "I don't think so."

"You look familiar." She studied his eyes.

"No, I would never forget you." He accepted her handshake. At a loss for words, he lingered in her grip and glanced over his lost love. Hidden beneath her lab coat was a vaguely familiar bulge. A baby bump.

She's a doctor and she's pregnant. Thank God, she's okay. Dr. Callahan, she married Jason.

"Sir, we have administered several tests and discovered a concern in your father's heart."

"How bad?" Shock rolled through him.

"It would appear he has been battling heart disease for many years. He had a mild heart attack, and there is some damage to the Coronary Vessels that supply blood to the heart."

"Can they be repaired?" Panic filled him.

"As luck would have it, we have been working on innovative treatments that have been proven in clinical studies to reverse a great deal of damage. There are no guarantees; however it's worth a try."

"I trust you, Ja— er, Dr. Callahan. Help my dad, please?"

"Of course. You are welcome to see him. His wife is with him. She's the one who brought him in. He was fortunate to have her there. Without prompt medical attention, it could have proven fatal."

"Thank you." He held his hand out once more for a final touch.

***

"DAD?"

"Son, come on in. I don't know what all the fuss is about. I'm fine." He lay propped up in the hospital bed with an oxygen tube up his nose.

Luther approached his bedside, shaken from worry. "I'm so thankful you're okay." He sat beside Jasper and took his hand.

"I'm all right, thanks to my sweetheart." He waved to the side, where, sitting somewhat disheveled in her pink velour tracksuit, was Beth. Her usual perfect bun of silver hair unkempt, and her flawless makeup had smudged, leaving raccoon like marks under her eyes.

"Thank you, Beth. I don't know what we would do without you."

"I'm so thankful he's alive. I thought I had taken such good care of him. We eat healthy and go for walks every day with Kiki."

"Mrs. Evans?" Jasmine entered the room with the clipboard.

"Yes, Doctor?"

"Please don't blame yourself. He will recover quickly because of how well you have taken care of him. Heart disease can go undetected for years."

"What do we do?"

***

"DINNER is served, Mr. and Mrs. Evans." Sarah stood at the parlor door.

"Thank you, dear." Beth stood up, with her long, white haired companion, Kiki, under her arm. "Please, won't you all accompany us to the dining room?"

Jasper joined her at the door and waited for their guests to join them.

Jasmine and Jason followed, hand-in-hand. Giselle came next, and Luther was the last to join the procession.

"Thank you so much for having us here for dinner." Jasmine's eyes lit up as she delved into the prime rib.

"It was our pleasure, and the least we can do for saving Jasper's life," Beth replied.

"Tell me, Jasmine, how far along are you, if you don't mind my asking?" Luther smiled at her.

Jason, at her side, held her hand on the table, and they stared at each other for a moment with wide grins.

"We're six months along," she cooed.

"It's your first child?" Jasper chimed in.

"Yes. She came along a year earlier than we planned." She giggled.

"It's a girl?" Beth's eyes lit up. "Oh, you must let me help shop for her."

"It would be an honor."

"Giselle, how's your dinner?" Jasper patted her hand.

"Lovely, thank you, sir."

"There's no need to call me sir. You're part of the family, my dear."

"I'm just a secretary." She tipped her head down and sipped on a glass of water.

"Giselle," Luther interrupted and peered across the table at her. "I beg to differ. You have been my biggest support in getting my business off the ground. You've been there through thick and thin and kept me on the honest path to success."

Her cheeks flooded with red. "You've been so good to me, Luther. You helped me out of a dark hole when...." She placed her glass down and wiped her mouth with her napkin.

"How long ago did it happen, Giselle?" Beth cocked her head and offered a gentle tone.

"About a year ago, in the Caribbean."

"What happened?" Jason glanced around the table with confusion.

"Her son, Marvin, passed away."

"I'm so sorry, I had no idea." He covered his mouth.

"It's okay. I'm much better, thank you. We haven't been close in a very long time."

"Do you mind my asking how?" Jasmine's voice was but a whisper.

"He had just won the Powerball lottery, forty-three million dollars."

"Wow!" Jason's jaw dropped.

"Well, he left everyone behind and moved to the Cayman Islands. Not even so much as a goodbye." She gritted her teeth.

The room went deathly silent, all eyes falling on Giselle.

"I always said he spent too much time worried about money and not enough time caring about others. He found himself a teenybopper cover model and married her on the beach" She tsked with disgust. "Sent me a picture on the cell phone."

"What happened next?" Jason prompted her.

"Karma, I suppose."

"What do you mean by that?" Jasmine asked.

"Well, after the first night of their honeymoon, she took off with a yoga instructor and emptied out his Cayman Island's bank account. He was so distraught, he actually sent me a message." She huffed. "Asking me for money. I didn't have any since he stole my nest egg before he left."

"That's terrible," Jason scoffed.

"Luther helped me get it all back."

"How did you get money back from him?" Jasper arched his brows.

"I just handled things the way you would have, Dad. Don't worry about it." He winked. *Cost me a bundle, but she's looked after and has all that she needs.*

"Well, imagine my surprise when I got a call from the local authorities the next day. They found him dead." Giselle sighed and let her shoulders slump.

"What happened?"

"It would seem Marvin had gone for a walk, barefoot on the beach, and waded into the water. From what they said, he stumbled upon a smack of jellyfish."

"Oh, my word." Jasmine gasped.

"The coroner report said he got stung over fifty times. Death by jellyfish."

Luther chewed the inside of his mouth to hold back the chuckle lingering inside. "Karma can be pretty harsh."

"It would seem so." Jason shook his head.

"Beth, dear." Jasper tapped his chin with his fingers. "Didn't you date him a while back?"

"Oh, heavens, I did. He went to Mexico, and I never heard from him again."

"How did you and Jasper meet, Mrs. Evans?" Jasmine continued to cut up her meat, and the knife scraped alone the bone china. Luther cringed at the ear piercing noise.

"Sorry," she smiled sheepishly.

"Can't come between a pregnant lady and a meal." Luther nodded and passed her the gravy.

"We met through Luther." Beth grinned and patted Jasper's hand. "Before he left, Marvin had tried to get me to invest in some stocks. After I hadn't heard from him, I grew suspicious and went to his office and met Luther. Thank goodness he saved me from that foolish investment. After he got me all squared away financially, he introduced me to his father, and we haven't been apart since."

"You're married?" Jason pointed to her princess-cut diamond ring.

"We are. Within six months of our introduction, we just knew we were right for one another, and here we are, happy as can be."

Luther pulled his wallet out and rested it on his lap under the table. He took out an old photo of his mother, smiled, and winked at it. *Just like I promised, Mom.*

"Jasmine is a cardiac surgeon. Tell me, Jason, what do you do?" Giselle chimed in.

"I'm an artist."

"Come now, Jason, don't be so modest," Beth sang. "You, my darling young man, are a genius."

"I wouldn't say that."

"Oh, heavens, yes you are. That is the other reason I've asked you both here to dinner."

Jason pulled his shoulders back and watched her. "What do you mean?"

"I had the divine privilege of viewing your recent collection at the Museum of Modern Art."

"You did?" He shifted in his chair with wide eyes. "What did you think of it?"

"Jason, I have been looking for a worthy cause to invest in for years. I believe in paying it forward. Without children of my own, I wanted to be sure I'd have a legacy to leave behind. Art has always been near and dear to my heart."

"Mine, too." He collected his wine glass and took a long sip.

"I plan to start up a special school for budding artists, and I'm looking for a skilled professional, such as yourself, to be the head of the art department."

"Me?" He choked on his drink. "You want me?"

"I want the best, and from what I have seen, you are it."

"I don't know what to say, Beth." He looked to Jasmine, and she nodded.

"Yes, baby, this is such a wonderful opportunity for you."

"Monday at eleven o'clock, you can meet me at Luther's office, and we will arrange all the details." Beth smiled and sipped her red wine.

Chapter Twenty-Six

"GOOD MORNING, Mr. Evans." Giselle followed him into his office and put his briefcase on the desktop.

"Good morning, sunshine. It's a beautiful Monday. How did the rest of your weekend go?"

"Just lovely. I went out on a date." She beamed.

"With someone who will treat you like a queen, I hope?" He walked back to her.

"Oh, he is such a kind man."

"I'm glad to hear it." Luther patted her arm then returned to his desk and took a seat in his plush leather chair.

He fumbled through his stacks of legal files and searched for one in particular. Just as he found it at the bottom, he pulled it out, and Giselle returned to the room. The pile toppled over onto the desk.

"I'm sorry to disturb you, Mr. Evans," She rushed over and helped him tidy the unsightly mess. "I know she doesn't have an appointment, but there is a very attractive lady outside. She asked to meet with you as soon as possible."

"When is my first meeting?" He glanced at his Timex watch.

"Not until eleven o'clock, sir."

"Sure. Please show her in." Luther straightened his tie and stood up. "Oh, Giselle?"

"Yes, sir?"

"Did she say what her name is?"

"Angela Arch."

He tilted his head with curiosity. "Fine, let her in."

Luther sucked in a sharp breath at the vision of the magnificent creature who stood at the doorway. The woman was the shimmering image of regal beauty. The sheen of her hair held the rich copper tones of the sunset and trailed in a neat ponytail down her left shoulder. She stood, draped in long over coat of azure blue, and wore on her left lapel an intricate silver eagle. In her hand glimmered a gold clutch bag, encrusted in jewels.

"Gabrielle?"

"Thank you, miss." She nodded to Giselle and pulled the door shut behind her.

"Is that really you?" His pulse raced.

"I hear you've made good on some promises in the last five years." She strolled up to the chair on the opposing side of his bureau and took a seat with a sultry smile.

"Is this a dream...again?" He walked around the desk and sat against the tabletop as he studied her beautiful face.

"No, it's not a dream." She reached over and pinched his hand.

"Ouch!" He shrunk back from the minor sting.

"Just confirming for you." She nestled into her chair and folded one leg over the other.

"Angela Arch, huh?" He chuckled. "Meaning, my exquisite archangel?"

"Still sharp as a whip, I see." She winked.

"What are you doing here?" A wave of panic shot through him. "Oh, God. Am I in trouble again?"

"No, in fact, Luther, you've done well, very well."

"I haven't seen you since Mexico."

"You had completed your tasks, and once you were granted redemption, I got reassigned to another case."

"Sounds very formal. Anyone interesting?"

"Every charge has their unique traits."

"Was he as cute as me?"

"*She* was a beautiful girl, who needed guidance." Gabrielle stood up, face-to-face with Luther, and lingered close enough he could feel the warmth of her breath brush across his lips.

"Still tempting me to blasphemy, I see." Although it took every ounce of self-control he possessed, he resisted stealing a kiss.

"As you may well remember, Luther, entrapment is not my style." She reached beside him and placed her bag on the desk then inched back from kissing range.

"What brings you to this part of the world, angel?"

Gabrielle wandered around his office and inspected his pictures, furnishings, and the whole layout of the room. "I heard about this." She pointed to the framed newspaper article on the wall. "You formed an extension of the fraud task force, geared to women of wealth?"

"I did."

"You educate them on how to protect themselves from scamming Romeo's who are out to bilk their fortunes?"

"I do."

"Impressive."

"Really?" He loosened his restrictive necktie. "Why do I get the feeling there is a punch line coming?"

"I don't know." She moved onto the next article.

"I understand you single-handedly uncovered investment fraud here in your own brokerage for a few measly millions."

"True."

"And, you introduced Beth and your father. Now, they are married and living full lives?"

"I promised my mother I would."

"You encouraged Beth to open an art school and got Jason a job?"

"I did." He gave a one-sided grin.

"And you paid back every single penny Marvin stole from his mother and Beth with your own money?"

"It's the least I could do."

"Luther, I'm proud of you." She turned around.

"Why is that?"

"You did all this after you were granted redemption. You could have easily moved on with your life and started anew."

"But I needed to make things right for everyone. Dad and Beth have each other. Giselle has her money back and a purpose, and people that accept her as family."

"Your actions are very noble."

Luther hesitated then crossed his arms over his chest. "Gabrielle, you're kinda freakin' me out."

"Why?"

"Because I get the nagging suspicion you have an agenda with me."

"What would make you think that?" She gave a playful pout.

"Because I haven't seen you since the jail cell in Mexico."

"I know. I missed how much you irritated me." She smirked.

"So, you're here because you missed me?"

"In a sense."

"Are we back to the whole talking in tongues business?"

Gabrielle drew in a deep inhale, expelled it, and gave a pout. "I'm here to ask if you can give me a little guidance this time."

Skeptical, Luther stared at her. Her narrowed his eyes and pursed his lips. "You want my guidance?"

"As a matter of fact, yes." She walked to him, standing face-to-face, lingered, and then sat down again.

"Okay, princess." He returned to his side of the desk, removed his jacket, hung it over the back of his chair, and sat down. Luther undid his cuffs, rolled up his blue cotton sleeves, and rested his forearms on the desk. He shot her a stern glare. "Please, tell me you're about to ask me about investments, exchange rates, or a simple problem I'm actually good at."

She cupped her hands together over her jittery knee and shook her head.

"How to track down a dishonest scum bag?"

She shook her head again and smirked.

"How to...." He glanced up at the ceiling, his smart-ass comments ran thin. "Report fraudulent activities?"

"Not even close."

Rising, Luther peered out the large office window and up at the sky.

"What are you doing?" She giggled.

He ran his fingers through his hair and flexed his jaw muscles. "Looking for rolling clouds."

"Why?"

"I'd like to know when the lightning is gonna strike me down." He glanced back at her.

"You really are paranoid, aren't you?" She folded her arms across her chest.

"For real, angel. What's this about?"

Gabrielle gripped the arms of the chair, uncrossed her leg, and steeled her back. "Have you had any experience in career counseling?"

"Me?"

"Yes."

"No, why?" He spun around and faced her.

"I find myself at a crossroads, as of late and need to explore new options."

"Gabrielle, what happened? Did you get...do angels get fired?"

"No, we don't."

"So then?" He crinkled his brows and hunched up his shoulders.

"After careful consideration, and a long discussion with Metatron, I expect to take a—" She glanced away from him.

"What?" He stepped forward and held his palms up with irritation.

"A sabbatical."

"From the rank of archangel? Is that even possible?" Luther's knees wobbled.

"Yes. It isn't common, but it can be done."

"So, if you leave, there's no Archangel Gabrielle to help people with healing and love?"

"They would find a substitute to replace me."

"Are you serious?"

"Yes."

"For how long?"

"Not long. Maybe fifty years or so."

"Why would you want to take an angelic sabbatical? Is work that tough?"

"The job is manageable, but...."

"I'm all ears." He tucked his hands in his dress pant's pockets.

"My desires have been steering me in a different direction these past few months."

"What desires?"

"I've found myself distracted, and at times, disinterested while guiding my charges."

"Archangel burnout? That's new."

"Not at all, Luther. From time to time, under extenuating circumstances, we can be allotted an opportunity to live among the human population, in mortal form, and experience a different existence."

"Other archangels have done this?"

"A few."

"And their substitutes just pick up where they left off?"

"Essentially."

Luther walked around the desk, pulled his chair around, and sat facing her. "What experience do you want, Gabrielle?"

In silence, she reached up and traced her finger along the deep scar of his lip and cheek.

"You're just messing with me." He hesitated from his impulse to pull back.

"No, Luther. I can't stop thinking about you."

"Metatron will have my head on a platter for swaying you to the dark side," he chortled.

"Truth be told, in our review of my recent performance of duties, it was his recommendation."

Luther studied her luminescent eyes, the same beauty he cherished for a week, and memories he fought to keep over the last five years. Lost in the depth of azure, he leaned in to her, cupped the nape of her neck, and captured her lips with a gentle kiss. Her acceptance spurred him on, and their kiss grew impassioned.

After a few bliss-filled moments, Luther retreated and stared at her.

"What is it?"

He glanced out the window again at the clear blue sky. "Entrapment is not your style, right?"

"Right."

Luther stood up and held his hand out for her to accept.

"Where are we going?"

"If I'm gonna commit blasphemy, the least I can do is buy you breakfast, angel."

The End

Other Kali Willows Stories You May Enjoy

Double Dragon Seduction

Dragon Temptation

Dragon's Breath

Dragon's Bond

Double Dragon's Blood Series (*in print-coming March 2015*)

Designing Passion

Tantric Storm

Terminal Lust

Damnation & Desire

Savannah's Ghost Tale

Shadowed Desires (*print anthology*)

Romancing the Author (*coming April 2015*)

Made in the USA
Charleston, SC
24 October 2015